Mere Chances

Veronika Simoniti

MERE CHANCES

SELECTED STORIES

Translated from the Slovenian by Nada Grošelj, with the
exception of "Aegeus" (translated by David Limon) and "The
True Story of Victor Lustig" (translated by Špela Bibič).

DALKEY ARCHIVE PRESS

Library of Congress Cataloging-in-Publication Data
Names: Simoniti, Veronika, author.
Title: Mere chances (selected stories) / Veronika Simoniti ; translated
by Nada Groselj, with the exception of "Aegeus" (translated by David
Limon) and "The True Story of Victor Lustig" (translated by Spela
Bibi.
Description: First Dalkey Archive edition | Dalkey Archive : Victoria,
TX, 2018.
Identifiers: LCCN 2017035413 | ISBN 9781628972375 (pbk. : alk.
paper)
Subjects: LCSH: Identity (Psychology)--Fiction. | Language and lan-
guages--Fiction. | Communication--Fiction. | Psychological fiction.
Classification: LCC PG1920.29.I46 A2 2018 | DDC 891.8/436--
dc23
LC record available at https://lccn.loc.gov/2017035413

www.dalkeyarchive.com
Victoria, TX / McLean, IL / Dublin

 Co-funded by the Creative Europe Programme
of the European Union

Dalkey Archive Press publications are, in part, made possible through
the support of the University of Houston-Victoria and its programs in
creative writing, publishing, and translation.

Printed on permanent/durable acid-free paper

Contents

The Names of Things   3

On the Mainland   14

Garda Stories   22

Patterns of the World   31

Cyrano   37

Comet Hunting   45

Aegeus   53

The True Story of Victor Lustig   59

Portugal   65

A House of Paper   72

Ramón de Caballo   80

Roma Termini   88

Remington Noiseless   95

Out of Oblivia   100

Jet Lag   107

The Feud   113

Olivija   121

The Rex   128

The Life and Death of Silent Silvina   139

Papilio Dardanus   145

Sixty Percent   154

The Names of Things

For Mr. Aldo

ILL-BODING CLOUDS ARE thickening above Veli Sunac, barges are returning to the little port, villagers and tourists are gathering under the thatched eaves of Jure's Bar. *Hey, Pop Ive, you said you hated cell phones, but just look at him gabbing away!—I hate them even worse now,* answers the white-haired fisherman, *worse than before,* and the group of young men in the bar brays laughter. Cats have already taken shelter under the canvases stretching over the fishing nets piled on the pier, the first raindrops plop against the concrete pier, then the rain pours down. Scattered through the village bay is a handful of stragglers, hurrying indoors.

Adela is curtaining off the pension terrace with vertical canvases, soon she will serve dinner. A lightning bolt traces a vein-like path through the sky, and thunder booms out moments later. *This summer's let us down and no mistake,* the landlord addresses a French family. *Isn't it always so rainy?* the French wonder. *No, this year's unusual,* says the landlord, *gazda,* shaking his head. When the air is quite frizzled with watery threads, Klaus comes cycling down the slope into the village, his dog running behind. He rides up to the pension, leans his bike against the rail, with *terra-rossa*-stained rivulets purling underneath, calls to the dog, *Come on, Platon,* and springs inside the house.

It's eight o'clock and the bar empties out, the only tables occupied are those at which accidental visitors are ordering dinner. On the other side of the bay, pension guests on the curtained-off terrace are waiting for heaped plates to arrive. A tractor driven by an old farmer comes rattling from the hill, his wife is sitting in the trailer dressed in black, a dark scarf on her head, they're returning from the field at the stroke of eight as usual. On the pension terrace looms up Aldo's mighty stature and a smaller man in its shadow, chatting and greeting the guests, nodding politely. *How important the names of things are,* Aldo is arguing with a puff on his pipe, *just think about it, we Dalmatians call a seagull a GAH-leb because it lands on a rock as fast as its name is short. But the Germans call it Möwe*—Aldo draws out the umlaut—*this word embodies its slow and dignified flight.* Aldo, the *gazda*'s brother, who only comes to Veli Sunac in the summer and spends the rest of the year in Paris, luxuriously puffs smoke from his mouth, following it with his eyes. *Oh yes, how important the names of things are,* thinks Adela, listening to Aldo's ruminations through the clack of cutlery, Ante promised last night to take her to a dance on the other side of the island but never showed up. The word *invitation* is understood differently by men. There's that Austrian calling for her again, what does he want now, what's he finding fault with again, yesterday he wanted his plate warmed up, today he won't have seasoned salad, in fact he's in the habit of bringing from his room a picnic basket and taking out his own balsamic vinegar, Austrian beer, and toast. Adela stops by his table, fixing a smile on her lips. *Was machst du heute abend,* Klaus asks. *Dear God, not another invitation,* thinks Adela. *Schlafen,* she retorts, moving away from the table, *allein,* she adds without looking at him. Just to avoid any misunderstanding: the word *alone* has a single meaning. As if to confirm her thought, lightning strikes quite close to Veli Sunac.

The next morning is gray again. *Crazy summer,* says the *gazda* to the French family who have come to breakfast, *Isn't it normal for a drop or two to fall in this season,* wonder the French again, *No, no, this year's crazy, the weather's been nothing but lousy,* the pension owner shakes his head. The grass has never been so green, there are normally fewer flies and mosquitoes, and mildew is flourishing in all the rooms. From the house comes waddling to the terrace a crumpled Klaus with the dog at his heels. *Oh, breakfast is served here so early*, he grumbles in the direction of the French family, but the father just shrugs. *I was going to cycle about twenty kilometers today, but the weather's not looking up. Care for a coffee at Jure's? I'm certainly not going to offer you any sour Dalmatian booze. How come they can't concoct a decent wine?* The French and Klaus, followed by the dog, walk up to the counter of Jure's Bar. *The only eyesore around here is our pension.* The French chuckle, *Have you heard about the Monsieur who ate at the Eiffel Tower every day because it was the only point in Paris from which you couldn't see that monster of a construction. Heh heh heh.*

Adela clears the breakfast tables and a couple of minutes later she is already marching down the other side of the bay. *Where are you in such a rush to, Adela?* asks the bearded postman, Stipe, hanging out the window of his office. *I'm really pressed for time, there's no one at the pension to help, I'm quite alone.—What? What did you say?* Stipe calls after her. *I'm alone!* yells Adela. *Me too*, Stipe sighs jokingly, and the old geezers sipping their beer in front of the store guffaw. Then Adela enters the village store, where Ante works. Ante beckons her over two German customers to join him behind the counter. *Sorry about last night, Mario stopped by.—What sort of deals are you running with that Mario, is he ever going to fix you up with a job on the mainland?* Ante raises his eyebrows as if to say, *Who can tell?*

In the twinkling of an eye, the air is dotted with pearly droplets. From Jure's Bar, the father of the French family is watching the Mediterranean village, which lines the little bay with about thirty houses. *The rain gives it the look of a Breton hamlet*, he thinks, nodding to the chatting Austrian who has been deprived of his cycling tour by the rain. *Mediterranean laziness aside, they don't really know savoir vivre, as you call it.*

*In fact this phrase is untranslatable, just like condition humaine,
some words simply have to keep their original names.* The French
mother is sipping at her coffee, listening to Klaus in disbelief.
Klaus's dog is lying on the floor, gnawing at a fake bone. The
conversation is cut short by a flash, followed by a clap of thunder. Startled, the dog barks. *Shut up, Platon! Damn, what's this
crap, anyway?* exclaims Klaus. *Donnerwetter,* replies Jure. *Did you
know that Benjamin Franklin actually channeled lightning along
a wire that was stretched from a child's kite to the earth?* asks the
head of the French family in a weighty tone. *But Papa, how is
lightning made,* asks the French tyke. *H'm, it hasn't been fully
explained . . . —How do you know that, are you a meteorologist?*
asks Klaus. *No, a physicist.—Well, then, how is lightning made,*
Klaus repeats the question. *The whole cycle begins with the separation of charges in the thundercloud,* replies the French father,
*just imagine, they even tried to explain this phenomenon by flying
airplanes through the clouds.—Quel courage,* remarks the French
lady. *It was discovered that the top of a thundercloud, six or seven
kilometers above the earth, has a positive charge, while the lower
part, at a height of three to four kilometers, is negative. The charge
carried by the lower part of the cloud is strong enough to cause a
difference in voltage between the surface of the earth and the lower
level of the cloud, a difference amounting to twenty, thirty, or even
up to a hundred million volts. Imagine, an ordinary battery has
just one and a half volts,* adds the Frenchman, turning to his
little son. *Madame* pats the boy's head. *Then large electric fields
lead to the ionization of the air and to an electric breakthrough,*
continues the Frenchman. *At the breakthrough, the negative ions
from the cloud's base streak to the earth's surface in the form of
a lightning flash. But if we want to understand how lightning is
made, we should explain first how the separation of charges comes
about.—The separation of charges?* echoes Klaus. *Mais oui, that's
the phenomenon when parts of a thundercloud are charged differently at different levels.—Interesting, interesting,* nods Klaus, and
the French *Madame* casts an admiring glance at her husband.

Rising, Klaus makes his way to the counter with Platon trailing behind. Scanning the customers, he is approached by Aldo. *You know,* Klaus speaks up, *it's a real treat for me to make up stories about people I haven't got a clue about. The fat girl over there came in a long limo with American license plates, she must be an emigrant, a native of Veli Sunac. Then the ugly Italian, you see, that's not his wife but his mistress, no, better still, a girl he's paid to go cruising with him in his revolting yacht.* Aldo gives a good-natured chuckle. *Imagination helps me with my TV work, with interviews, continues Klaus, you know, empathy and all that.—I use special methods in my line, too,* explains Aldo. *Have I told you about the tree exercise?—Tree? Aren't you a logopaedist?* wonders Klaus. *Sure, sure, but look, that tree exercise is so much fun: I told a group of Croatian kids who knew no foreign languages that a tree was called different things in different languages: tree, albero, Baum, arbre, etcetera. Then I drew a sharply pointed tree, and everyone said it was called a tree. But in another group I drew a tree with a nicely rounded top, and almost everyone agreed that it was called Baum.—Oh, I see, it's the image of the idea that determines the name,* Klaus observes.

The rain is drenching the pavements and piers. Adela and Ante are standing under the eaves of Ante's house. *But have you told Mario about my condition?* asks Adela. *Not yet,* he replies. Adela looks at him with concern, double concern, it's four eyes that look at him with concern because Adela is carrying another pair under her heart. Her throat constricts, *He's totally irresponsible, how am I supposed to have a child with him,* and she runs down to the sea. The rain is plastering her dress to her body, tingling raindrops are sliding from her heavy hair and down her face. Reaching the end of the biggest pier, the jetty where the Lovrijenac used to land, she gazes at the surface of the sea riddled with holes by skywater. *Once upon a time people believed that everything came from the sea,* so they were told in high school by their mainland teacher. Following after her, Ante steps up close and embraces her from behind. *If it's a son, we'll call him Ivica, what do you say?—No, no, Ivica is so mousy gray, his name must be blue, with a whiff of the sea*, says Adela.

The day passes in a murky drizzle and the evening finds the pension guests at their tables again. Adela is carrying plates and the old couple comes rolling downhill in their rattling tractor, in defiance of the weather. Klaus is reading a tourist guide to Dalmatia, the French family is playing cards, others are chatting. The landlord is grilling meat. His brother Aldo struts across the terrace, wishing a good evening to all. *They're sticking around because they hope it'll clear up sooner or later*, he thinks, *but not this year, I'm afraid.—A penny for your thoughts?* asks Klaus. *Ah, nothing, nothing, I was just thinking about . . .—About the summer*, Klaus chips in. *How can you know that?—Well*, continues Klaus, *you were saying to yourself how dumb these foreigners are, paying for a holiday and hoping from day to day that a new day may bring fine weather. But you're convinced there'll be no sun this year.—He's reading from my head*, says Aldo to himself but is at once startled by the fear that Klaus might read that thought as well. *Depends on what we imagine under the word sun, or the word summer, or the word holiday*, Klaus goes on. *For us Austrians, these concepts mean something else than for you, of course. You enjoy yourselves slowly, in the rhythm of sages, and shrink from scorching light, while we scamper after sunrays. We, for instance, feel it's easier to strike up new friendships in the summer, in warm places. We relax, and the sea and wine do their job, too. We come here to fall in love. I, for instance, have fallen for your Adela over the last few days. And that's something I'd never dare to admit in Graz to anyone I'd known just for a week, as I've known you. And I'll tell you another thing: do you know what I'd give my life for? I'd die for the idea of lo . . .* At this point there's a crash, a peal of thunder, and Klaus's word is drowned in heaven's boom. Platon whines. *Yes, that's what I'll disappear for*, adds Klaus when the only sound left is the patter of rain against the awning stretched above the terrace.

The next morning is partly cloudy for the locals or partly clear for the foreign guests. Adela is bringing slices of fragrant, hot toast to the tables. The French family is looking at an island map, planning a hike, the other tourists are sleepily squinting at the day. Klaus hasn't surfaced yet. After breakfast, Adela hurries to the store to see Ante. They withdraw to the back room used for storage. *Well?* asks Adela, and Ante scratches his ear. *Looks like I'll get a job, but not officially.—What do you mean, not officially?—Eh, Mario can't register me, get it?—No, I don't get it.* A black cloud darkens Adela's brow. Will she ever manage to escape from her cherry orchard of long and windy, gray and idle winter days to the mainland? Her body longs for life even though it carries life inside, her eyes long for teeming chaos, her ears for the city hubbub.

Over the day, the mischievous sun will peek from the clouds at times to caress the island but soon hide away, shy. Nevertheless, the French return pleased with their hike and regale the landlord with tales of all they've seen. The landlord lights a fire to grill fish. *What's a fish called in French?—Poisson.—Poo-ah-zon?—Goodness, no, that means poison.* The guests sit down to their tables and Adela totes a heavy tureen to the terrace, greeting them courteously. The loyal tractor with the aged farmer couple comes huffing to the bay again, its rattle only drowned out by the rumble of the approaching storm. Lightning flashes twice in the distance. *Look, Papa, this flash was different from the first.—Yes, the first was forked lightning and the second chain lightning, but there's something called ball lightning as well.—Do lightning bolts have names too, Papa?—Yes, now that's really interesting, just think about it,* confirms the French dad. *Apart from bolts in the troposphere, some flashing phantoms were spotted in the nineties above the thunderclouds, at heights from fifty to ninety kilometers. These earned the ingenious names of elves and trolls. Since the atmosphere at such heights is thinner, lightning absorbs fewer molecules, that's why it's hardly visible to the naked eye. And it glows in various colors like ordinary de-electrifications, mostly in the color red.—Elves and trolls, Papa?—Yes, but even more enigmatic than the elves and trolls are the blue jets and the sources of gamma and X-rays, more electric phenomena high above the thunderclouds. And just imagine, the electrons of the elves rarely exceed the energy of twenty electron volts but the production of gamma rays calls for a million electron volts, that's the same ratio as between the power of a chemical explosive and that of an A-bomb.*

Klaus's table is as empty as it was at breakfast and Platon is nowhere in sight, either, notes Adela, *but that's all for the best, at least he won't nag again.* She looks toward the pension entrance and sees that his bike is no longer leaning against the rail. He must have cycled away on one of his island tours and missed dinner. She and Ante are going tonight to an outdoor concert in a nearby village. Once the tourists finish their meal and Adela tidies up the terrace, she goes to her room and puts on her makeup. She dons a seductive black dress; she can still afford it because her tummy isn't protruding yet. There's a storm raging outside but they said the concert would be held in any weather. Then it turns ten o'clock, Ante hasn't shown up, and Adela is seething with resentment.

*

Two days later, the morning sun shines forth in all her clearness, the bay is ringing with children's laughter, people are glancing contentedly around the fishing village, now utterly transformed and amiable. To their surprise, the guests on the pension terrace are confronted by a couple of policemen. The landlord hastens to explain that there's no cause for uneasiness, the policemen are just going to ask a few questions. About Klaus. When did they see him last, did anything strike them as odd, what did he talk about, did he hint that something was amiss, where was he planning to go? After the interrogation, the pension owner invites the two minions of the law for a glass of *loza*, grape brandy. *Lenić*, says one, stretching out his hand, *Benić*, introduces himself the other, and both shrug as if to say, *We know it sounds ridiculous but those are our names.—We've spotted nothing unusual in the replies of your guests, now give us the key to the Austrian's room.* Washing the glasses, Adela glances surreptitiously after the policemen. *A rum affair, this disappearance*, says the *gazda* to his brother Aldo. The policemen come back and beckon to Adela. Her blood rises. They sit down to the table in the landlord's kitchen. *Now we'd like to hear your story, too*, says Lenić. *My story?* wonders Adela. *Your story*, repeats Benić. *Well, that Klaus was, is, our guest, I saw him last three days ago.—Where did you see him?* asks Lenić. *At dinner.—But not again?* asks Benić. *No.* Silence. Lenić and Benić exchange looks, Lenić heaves a deep sigh. *What about this, Miss? We've found it in the Austrian's room*, says Benić, while Lenić fishes from his pocket a Polaroid snapshot featuring Klaus and Adela, with Klaus's room as the background and with a date in the bottom left corner, the date of three days ago. Adela freezes.

I was waiting for Ante that evening, Ante's my boyfriend, he works at the store . . . he promised to take me to a concert but never showed up . . . I was angry because he'd stood me up again, it wasn't for the first time . . . I was really mad, I'd have done anything to get back at him . . . Benić lays his cap on the table, scratching the top of his head. *I didn't want him to catch me waiting for him desperately . . . so I stepped out of my room . . . and Platon came strolling by.—Platon? Someone we haven't interrogated yet*, Lenić remarks to Benić, concerned. *Platon is Klaus's dog, that's how we struck up a chat in the first place . . . —With Platon?—No, with Klaus, he was coming after Platon, I asked him why his dog was called Platon. Klaus had been keeping out of sight all that day, he didn't come to dinner either, so I asked him where he'd been. He just said that he'd left experimentally but that he was going to leave for real the next day.—What did he mean by it?* asks Lenić. *He wouldn't tell me*, answers Adela, *but then we took a picture of us, just for fun, that's where this photo comes from.—Well, and why, why is the Austrian's dog called Platoon?* inquires Benić. *It's Platon, after the Greek philosopher Plato,* explains Adela, *Plato believed that ideas were more real than natural phenomena, so Klaus told me.* Now it's Lenić's turn to scratch his head. *Well, he claimed that all natural phenomena were just shadows of eternal forms and ideas,* continues Adela. Lenić and Benić exchange glances, the company at the table is joined by Aldo. *But what's that got to do with the Austrian's disappearance?* wonders Lenić. *I don't know, I'm just telling you what went on and what we talked about the last evening when I saw Klaus, he was telling me about Plato's world of ideas.—That's right,* it dawns on Aldo, *he said the same thing to me, that the idea determines the name, interesting, how interesting.*

Benić heaves a deep sigh, Lenić rolls his eyes. *Look, you'll catch on at once, I'll explain in a jiffy: do you know what a seagull is called in German?* asks Aldo. *What tricks are you up to, you folks, that's not normal,* Lenić interrupts with a raised voice, *we want facts! Facts, get it? What are you hiding, why are you trying to lead us by the nose with some sort of ideas?—Though Klaus agrees more with Aristotle, who claimed just the opposite,* continues Adela. *And what did this other fellow claim?* asks Lenić. *That the real thing comes before the idea,* expounds Adela, *and Klaus believes that you can only name a thing once you've seen it or felt it, that the naked idea has no name by itself, you're the one who names it.—Who, me?* asks Benić. *That's enough,* cuts in Lenić, *we won't learn anything here,* he pushes back his chair and rises, *come on, let's go.* It's only when they've clambered into their blue car that Adela sighs with relief and Aldo lets out a guffaw. At that very moment Platon comes running into the pension, wagging his tail.

The sun is beating down in glorious conflagration and Adela is trying to order her thoughts. Here is the heartbeat of the budding baby inside her, here is Ante—*oh, that bumpkin of an*

Ante!—here is her yearning for the mainland, here on her still lingers the smell of Klaus's body from three nights before.

The only one with a clear head is Aldo. He has found out what Klaus wanted to say on the evening when he was drowned out by thunder. He knows what Klaus would have died for. And when Lenić and Benić come the next day to tell the chilling news, Aldo understands everything, *He was killed by lightning*, says Lenić, *on Lunina Planota, the charred body was transported yesterday to the mainland and then on to Austria*, adds Benić. And while a *Möwe* is hovering above the sea surface with wings spread out, a white and gray *GAH-leb* swoops down to perch on a cliff.

On the Mainland

I HAD IT PACKED in a modest travel bag of Pompeian red, firmly wedged among the other stuff on the passenger seat. By no means should it topple over, it would have been somehow sacrilegious even though it was tightly, one might say hermetically, closed. Now and then its presence sent a shiver down my spine, slight but still chilling, its closeness gave my trip a meaning, a purpose, and a stamp of lead, but took away my appetite in the very country where one eats so well.

Petra had said that she wanted to end up in some pretty place but she never told me what she had in mind, either because her time had run out or because of her secrecy, which she'd developed into an attitude in the end. As I knew her inside out, I thought first of Provence and then of Tuscany, and since Tuscany is closer, I decided on the latter. Sitting down in her old Clio I set out . . . toward Petra's grave.

She'd said that she would like to be scattered and I told her jokingly that she already was scatty because she kept forgetting things, I said so because I had to lighten somehow the weight of those last months. Under a tree, in a meadow, in the sea, where, Petra? *In some pretty place, nothing more, just some pretty place*, she said. She never considered what it would take to persuade the authorities that I wanted to carry out the rite myself: by law it can only be done by authorized institutions, complete with all the trimmings, all the pomp and distasteful scenery. I've never understood why one should be stuck into the soil, it's not as if we had to return there, after all, we hadn't crawled into the world from mud like worms. Even to scatter the ashes in the sea, I'd have to contact a specialized firm and bear the sight of trimmings which were not mine. In short, at funerals I hate all the painful and sadistic details thought out by the living with poor taste. There'll be nobody to answer to, your parents are gone, we have no children, I'm your husband, the only one entitled to claim you, so I filched the urn when it was set on the marble counter by a man in a black suit, a tie to match, and an absurd dark cap with a glittering shade, a man who said, *Just a moment, I'll go and enter the funeral for Tuesday.* Stashing the urn under my jacket lapel I legged it from the crematorium, at first warily, with mincing steps, then like one chased by imps and devils.

When I drove up to the border, the customs officer on the Slovene side merely glanced at my papers while his Italian colleague waved me on without a glance. I don't want to imagine what would have happened if they'd searched my car. What's in that container, sir? Eh, nothing special, just my wife's ashes.

Night was falling, the heavy, sultry air pressing through the half-open car window, I could smell the sea as I drove in complete darkness through Mestre, past the signs for Venice. My wife was quiet, shut up in her metal canister she was traveling on the passenger seat, for the first time forbearing from comments on my driving. *Say something, damn it,* I said aloud but turned on the radio at once, to keep my words from dissolving senselessly above the wheel and leading me astray. Like a ball, the moon's orangey globe hung low above the flat landscape, clustered round by the all-knowing stars. *Solo tuuuuu,* a man's cracked voice was singing on the radio, only you, Petra, indeed, only you, my only, my last, and I your last, too.

On the broad bypass road I decide at the last moment not to take the highway. Following a semicircular curve down from the overpass, I swing onto a smaller road. At first choked by the crowded houses, it runs hemmed in by two canals wafting the smell of seaweed and lined by poplars, trees I've never liked because they remind me of hateful childhood places. It's time for dramatic radio news, followed by ecstatic ads and at last a laid-back pop song, a woman's voice this time. I don't know why I'm crying all of a sudden, I thought I was past that stage, drained of all inner liquids.

The road is ripping through a grassy plain, with the last house long left behind, and after an hour's drive or so, when I glimpse something big, really huge, I reflect that I must be dreaming, that I'm too tired, I must stop. I pull away from the road but the enormity is still there, the closer I get the less I believe my eyes, impossible, in the middle of the grassy plain lies an ocean liner sunk into the turf. A giant white whale with a black stripe, or at least it seems white and black at night, among the rustle of grass blades and grass ears, stuck in a swamp about a hundred meters away from the overpass by which I've arrived. I stop by the road, step out of the car, and the beast looms even larger. I wonder what strongman could have dragged it ashore and pounded it into the earth. Making my way across the meadow, I have to lift my feet high because my steps are hampered by the knee-high grass, I'm approaching the prodigy, the steel mass, the moun-tain-high, supernatural craft already towering above me.

Seen from close up, the mystery is profaned. The ship is actu-ally crouching in a narrow canal invisible from the road. Even mightier and even taller now, it spreads wide, rising steeply above me, beckoning me into the giant shadow thrown by a moon that looks more lemony now. Hey, Petra, flashes a thought through my mind, hey, old girl, can you imagine a more original spot for scattering ashes? Don't nag now, it's true you won't be resting in your native soil, but you didn't want that anyway, and if I've found a better spot than old worn Tuscany, where I bet just about every well-heeled American wants to be buried these days, just be quiet and listen to me for a change. If you don't actually believe that the home soil is lighter, then it doesn't matter where exactly you transform into new substances, you never were keen on the fatherland idea and all that patriotic crap. You know yourself that abroad is a place that's different, and the place where you're going certainly is different. Let me know, by the way, if there are any such words as *home* and *abroad* on the other side, and what I'd also like to know is what language your new friends are speaking. Oh, and maybe you could tell me if the dead really weep over the tears of the living at funeral farewells.

With my feet getting tangled in the matted grasses, I hurry back to the car. Taking my torchlight from the hold, I carefully lift the red travel bag from the seat. With a conspiratorial air, the white monster watches me trudging back. *Visintin Dockyard*, proclaims a nearby sign. Having found a footbridge to cross the Styx, I step on board and over the rope meant to safeguard the entrance, entering the ship's dark belly.

To-yon-conk, to-yon-conk, echo my footsteps as I tread the metal floor, lighting both my way ahead and the walls smelling of fresh varnish. Huge screws are gripping painted panels in a calculated order, coldly welcoming me to the ship's technological bowels. Green floor and gray walls, like a replica of grass and cloudy skies, Petra, I'm certainly not going to scatter you in here although this ship could take you sailing all over the world. Down a narrow corridor I come to a flight of steps, I walk up the steps to a higher story and from there to the deck, clambering up a metal ladder fixed to the wall and leading into the sky. The moon has dropped close to the ground, my shadow is long and deep. Here I am, on a ship on the mainland and yet surrounded by water, a stone's throw away from the sea and yet in a river branch, in the Po estuary. The rustle of living grass stirred by the night wind spreads all the way to the numbed ship, the warm water plashing over her cold steel. But there's still hope, she will be revived by the dockworkers, her entrails will be warmed by the engines, reborn, she will cleave the frothy curls, again raising her soft honk.

Now, though, I have the ashes to think of, the direction of the wind, the position of east and west, water and land, the fate of ashes when they fall on dry ground, the mush to which they turn when they get wet. It doesn't really matter, I'll consider nothing, just surrender to the southerly night wind and the ship's maze. The thick cable groans, the crickets hush for a second.

Tonight I am captain, my ship anchored in a muddy bed, I sit down on a wooden crate and close my eyes, the tide before me heaves up and down.

With sunrays darting out behind his back like a halo, I can't see his face. Rising, I nod a greeting. I can see him clearly now, leathery skin, gray hair stiff with salt. Not a sea-god come to give me good advice about the urn, as I would've wished. He nods back, smiling, then says something I don't understand. I let him know that I've no clue what he's talking about, but he nods at my car and at the road, points his finger into the distance and pretends to be turning a car wheel. Now I see, he wants me to drive him somewhere.

Five minutes later we're sitting in my car, the two of us in front, Petra at the back, riding into the unknown. From time to time he points me in the right direction, with a brief comment (I have a feeling he knows all the sides of this world, *Over there is the birthplace of the northerly and here of the icy mainland wind*, he seems to be saying), while I'm merely nodding. He introduces himself, his name is Gino. We arrive at a small fishing town, *Chioggia* is what the sign says, and pull up by the sea. Beckoning me to follow, my new acquaintance leads me to the second story of a house. Without a key he opens the door to an apartment, calling *Marisa*, he either lives here or at least knows the residents. Offering me a chair in a kitchen-cum-dining room, he goes to search elsewhere. The room is simple: scant, shabby furniture, a window overlooking the sea and a large dresser topped by the framed photo of an elderly woman, a black ribbon bound slantwise across it and a candle burning by the side, a miniature shrine. *Marisa!* rings the voice from the next room, and I suspect that Marisa may be the woman in the photo and that she may have died quite recently without my travel companion's knowledge. Then Gino reappears, shaking his head. He whirls about the kitchen, brewing coffee for me, then he sits down next to me and lights a cheap cigarette. His hands are coarse, with black-rimmed nails. I thrust my chin toward the little shrine, inquiringly, and Gino says, *Mamma.* His glance meets mine and there is perfect understanding in our brief eye contact, absolute sympathy, although Gino doesn't know who I'm smuggling in my car. We're dumbly sitting at the table, each gazing at his shallow coffee, the candle glimmering on the dresser, and then I suddenly start, remembering the urn left in the car, at the same time I'm enfolded by all the pain, overwhelmed by the full weight of a living person, and I realize the futility of all our attempts at blunting death when the corners of our world begin to crack and crumble. At that moment I hear the door opening and see a stripe of light spill into the room, there appears a woman, it must be Marisa. *Ciao . . . ciao,* they greet each other with a kiss, *ciao,* I join in, shaking her hand. Marisa and Gino start talking in a language that's beyond me, and after a while Gino motions me to rise. I take my leave of Marisa and we go back to my car. Fishing nets are drying in front of it, someone has just set a black case full of dead fish before the mooring post.

From the apartment we take the stairs down to the *riva* and the parking lot; to shake off the choking anxiety, I start singing on the way down, *Volare, o-o-o, cantare, o-o-o-o,* Gino joins in and we laugh, that's the only way we can communicate. Coming down, we head for the car, and when we're right there, I notice that the back door on the right is half open, I grab the handle, yank it wide and . . . the urn on the back seat . . . is gone . . . .

Rigor mortis, at first I freeze, then a warm breeze rises, I'm flooded by a wave of heat, and somehow I get the message through to Gino with gestures, touching my wedding ring, drawing a cross in the air, and with the words *donna, morta, urna.* Gino asks incomprehensible and impossible questions which I can't answer. I close my eyes and my eyelids become covers spreading over my gaze, my head spins as it did once when Petra and I danced to Dalmatian songs at the seaside. Gino asks the nearby fishermen who are cleaning and mending their moldering nets if they've seen anything, but they just shake their heads, glancing at me in surprise. Then Gino gives me a serious look and says, *Polizia,* I start nodding but then remember that I'd filched the darned urn and that the police isn't the best of ideas, *No!* I grab his forearm to stop him. He looks at me as if I'd lost my mind, I collapse on the ground which has, judging by the splotches, seen a great deal of life, and rake my fingers through my hair, ready to cry. Where are you, Petra, where have you vanished, they must prize you even after death or they wouldn't have stolen you, while I, the bloody idiot, left you all alone in a bag on the car seat.

Gino and I make several rounds of the *riva,* asking passers-by if they happened to see the thieves, soul thieves, who broke into the car. If someone told us which direction they'd taken, we'd go after them and maybe stumble on the container which they'd have tossed away, seeing that they had no use for its material content, let alone the spiritual one.

I drive Gino out of town to the dockyard because he's in a hurry to get back to work. I wait for the end of his shift in the rushes near the steel hull, burning one cigarette after another, with the wind scattering tobacco ashes through the air. Here I am on the mainland, by a canal leading to seas unknown, standing before the narrow throat of stagnant water in which a dead ship lies, looking at the dwarves trying to revive her as Lilliputians might have tried to revive Gulliver. If I'd scattered you here into the canal last night, you'd have been borne away to the watery expanses from which, according to reliable sources, no one has returned with any tangible information. And everything would have been all right. I'm so alone, Petra, so alone in this hassle, scared to death and feeling so old.

Hoping to find you by some miracle, I slept over at Gino's, that is to say, I spent the night there without closing an eye, watched from the dresser shrine by Gino's mama, lit by the glimmering flame and shaking her head, *figlio mio*, my child, you've really botched it this time, through the window came bouncing again that smug orange ball, jovial like fat men with their rolling laugh, *hee hee hee, ha ha ha,* and smirked at me: *Whatever happens, the tide will come again.*

The next day is Sunday, so Gino doesn't leave for the dockyard. After our morning coffee we make more inquiries on the coast, and then I say goodbye to the friend of those two once-in-a-lifetime days, the friend who didn't take me for a loony as another in his place might have done with good reason. Sitting down in my old Clio, I head for home. I've lost you, Petra, I've mislaid for good your everlasting smile and flyaway chestnut hair and all the rest that I can't talk about, all that must forever remain ours alone.

I drive along the leaden road while the huge ship, crouching alone in the grass like an abandoned limbo, sadly follows me with her stranded whale's blind eyes along the gently sloping overpass and to the other side, as if honking a mournful farewell. Say hello to the Styx, you hulk of a ship, and to all that belongs there, I'll see you again, certainly, some time.

Garda Stories

VANILLA ICE CREAM, SUMMER frocks, and Paolo Conte, says the Hungarian girl, Ildico, passing on the question: *And yours?*— *Mine, mine, mine*, ponders Bjørn, *Definitely Italian women, all of Kieślowski, and Queneau's Exercises in Style. It's your turn, Aleksandar, now tell us about your favorite three things in the world.* Aleksandar scratches his ear and answers, *Tarot card games, sex, and hermetic Italian poets, not necessarily in that order.* For Konstantin it's folk songs, historical grammar, and democracy.

Are you paying alla romana or all together? chips in the waitress. Chorusing *Alla romana*, all begin to fish for their wallets in their pockets and bags. *You two are still left*, Aleksandar warns Raji and Almut. *Port wine, being in love, unpredictability*, answers Raji. The German woman, Almut, is more cautious, *My kids . . . my husband . . . my home . . .*

Suffusing mists have settled over Lake Garda again, a steam-stuffed August is beating down, dulling the will to study. The course participants head for an Art Nouveau villa, the seat of the school, and sit down in the lecture room, a breathtaking wood-paneled hall. *Today we'll practice the subjunctive a bit*, explains the teacher, Gianluca. *You should know*, he continues, *that the use of the Italian subjunctive is a sign of refinement, this verbal mood is used to express emotions, feelings, wishes, doubt, etcetera.—A very human mood*, Bjørn whispers in Aleksandar's ear.

Gianluca, says Aleksandar after class, *we'd like to hear about your favorite three things in the world, too.—H'm, an interesting game,* starts Gianluca, looking at the ceiling, *Football, that goes without saying, Jarrett's* Bridge of Light, *and sleep. But if I could answer again, I'd say it was mostly stories. I could even say: stories, stories, stories.—What kind of stories,* wonders Ildico, *life stories or literature or romances? . . . —Simply stories, stories with countless possible plots and dénouements but only one actual plot and one dénouement, I'm curious why just that plot and that dénouement out of a thousand possibilities. Tell me, for instance, what your favorite three things are, and I'll tell you why, as far as I can make out, though I've only known you for a fortnight. Each of them must have a story at the bottom.—Vanilla ice cream,* answers Ildico, *because it reminds me of summers at my grandma's place in Pécs, of freedom from cares and of the first kiss from the neighbor's boy. Paolo Conte, because he's magical and because the first time I heard him, it was at an awesome party. And summer frocks, well, I'm not telling you why those.—Fine with me, but I'd enjoy guessing,* says Gianluca, *now Konstantin's folk songs, historical grammar, and democracy, those are really not hard to crack, no offence but if I were Ukrainian, I'd probably have the same favorites, in the Leaden Times I'd have buried my head in science or drunk myself under the table, as in that novel,* Moscow—Petushki.*—Ah, sonny,* counters Konstantin, *you're still young, it's not as simple as that. The folk songs because they were studied by a woman I'm still in love with, historical grammar because I must drill to the very marrow of words, how else could I tell the stories so dear to you, and democracy, well, that's not a hard one because I lost two brothers to totalitarianism.*

And how would you find out, asks Aleksandar, *that I love the tarot game because of the cards I use for divination, hermetic poets because of the scent exuded by one of Montale's poems, not to mention the third?—That's where the charm and allure is,* answers Gianluca, *in guessing.*

*

A man of sharp and stern features is strolling down the riva in the September light, his gravity accentuated by the beat of his walking stick. The morning was glorious, cloudy but calm at dawn. We passed Limone where the mountain gardens, terraced and planted with citron trees, offer a bountiful and neat view, so he describes that day in his famous travelogue. What he passes over is that on that very day, it was the year 1786, he met on the lakeshore a girl with her mother and struck up a conversation, which was hardly his practice. The young lady's name is Margherita (ah, what a coincidence!) and she vaguely reminds him of his quondam fiancée, Lili von Schönemann. He invites them to join him for dinner at the hotel, and the ladies accept. They dine together the next day, too, and finally the ever-bolder Johann Wolfgang invites them to accompany him on his visits to the Garda neighborhood. When the trips around the lake have come full circle, Johann Wolfgang and Margherita are already head over heels in love. The only snag is that the next day brings the unexpected arrival of Margherita's fiancé, Fausto Bosisio, from Milan. Johann Wolfgang clears out and continues on his Italian travels. It was an honorable retreat, or so he believes.

*

Raji sips at his port wine, fingering his cigarillos. *Stories are at the bottom of everything, even your own conception,* muses Gianluca. *That's right, I'm the best proof of it,* says Raji in a warm voice, lighting a cigarillo, *I'm Indian after my mother and Portuguese after my father, a bizarre story.—Do tell us,* young Ildico shines up. *Gianluca says that the charm and allure is in the guessing,* repeats Raji. Aleksandar has a brainwave, *If you're all so crazy about stories, we can play at the cigarette of truth, you know the game? A cigarette is passed around and everyone takes a drag but mustn't knock down the ash, and the one who spills it has to tell a mysterious but true story, or if not, the others put questions to him and he's got to answer honestly.—Konstantin and me don't even smoke*, complains Almut, and the idea falls rather flat.

*

On the terrace of his villa, Mr. Gabriele puffs out his chest, draws fresh air to the very bottom of his lungs, and straightens the black patch covering his right eye, or rather, the spot where his eye had been until his recent breakneck flight over Vienna. From the villa, the Vittoriale degli Italiani, emerges a servant and strides toward Mr. Gabriele, who is now lounging against the lake ballustrade. On a silver tray glinting in the sun he is carrying a white envelope. Picking it up, Mr. Gabriele sniffs at it. He shivers down his spine, and only he knows that it's not with delight. He opens the envelope and reads a woman's hand informing him that its author is coming to visit that very afternoon. Mr. Gabriele fixes his gaze on the tranquil water surface. *Tell the lady that I'm not at home this afternoon*, he orders the footman.

*

While the group of participants is waiting for the afternoon session, Almut pulls a camera out of her bag, shouting, *Move together, all of you, time for a group shot!—Are you saying, moans Raji, that you want to freeze us into Polaroid reality?* Ildico, Bjørn, Aleksandar, and Konstantin meekly assume their position. *You come, too, Gianluca*, calls Almut, and Gianluca pulls along Raji as well. *There's no escaping it*, he whispers in Raji's ear, *that's just why I love stories: stories don't freeze us like photos, stories spring alive with each reading and hearing, and each time a little differently.*

*

The truth in every country lies at the bottom of a well, and the depth of the well can only be measured when it has been emptied. I'm pointed toward the truth by prefects, ministers, even private citizens. So truth emerges—slowly but surely, the bald man with a jutting chin all but chops his words. *All the truth?* ventures the journalist with notebook and pen in hand. *Nobody ever learns all the truth, but I have a sixth sense,* retorts the authoritarian. *A sense that beggars definition,* he adds, and rises from his fin-de-siècle armchair because a woman has entered the room, a middle-aged woman in a wine-red wrap. *Claretta, darling, come join us,* exclaims the squat man, *This is journalist Ludwig,* he says, *and this is Miss Petacci.* Taking Miss Claretta by the elbow, he leads her to the other side of the richly furnished room. *Where were you last night?* he asks in a completely different, hard voice. Claretta's lips are motionless, her eyes silent. *You've forced me to have you trailed,* hisses her broad-shouldered lover, but Claretta tears herself loose and leaves.

Where were we? the famous man asks. *To conclude, our dear leader, tell us something about art,* begs the interviewer. *The greatest of all is architecture,* answers the balcony-jawed tyrant. *I admire tragedy as well, I began two plays myself but never finished them. They're works in which I tried to clarify my ideas for myself, so it was more important to sketch than to finish them.*—*Rumor has it that you immersed yourself in German literature thirty years ago,* remarks the journalist. *I've read* Faust, *both parts, Heine, Schiller,* answers the Duce. *And of the moderns?* Ludwig wants to know. *D'Annunzio's plays, Shaw, though I'm irritated by his extravagant bids for originality, or Pirandello, who in fact wrote Fascist drama because it describes the world as we want it, the world as our creation,* is the Duce's reply.

*

On Sunday the participants settle on a small beach close to Mussolini's former villa. *These places are full of stories*, explains Gianluca at the sight, *Goethe traveled here, Carducci wrote poems on this lake, D'Annunzio lived here, and Mussolini fled here and established the Republic of Salò after capitulation.—Do you know any of those stories in detail?* asks Konstantin. *Of course*, confirms Gianluca and launches into Goethe's meeting with Margherita, D'Annunzio's refusal to see Eleonora Duse, and the revelation that Mussolini's mistress had mysteriously disappeared during his interview. *But something's missing from all these stories, there's always something left unexplained or unfinished*, complains Ildico. *Now you're going to dance to my fiddle*, laughs Gianluca, *it's you who should finish them.—Us? How?* wonders Bjørn. *The rule of the game is*, says Gianluca, *we stroll down the riva and listen to the passers-by, that's what your conclusions should derive from.*

The vapors have cleared up, the evening is warm, lemon-scented. *We were ripped off in that joint over there*, says the first passer-by, *Where did you buy this?* asks a lady, *Three of our neighbors died last year*, laments a third tourist, *Everyone has a price*, remarks an elderly gentleman. Gianluca, Aleksandar, Bjørn, Ildico, Konstantin, and Almut are sitting on a parapet before an ice cream parlor, eavesdropping. *Everyone has a price*, Raji rises to the bait, *that's what Margherita's fiancé Fausto Bosisio says when he arrives at the hotel, only to learn that Margherita is at dinner with a German gentleman. The next day he pretends that nothing is wrong and puts no questions to his naive fiancée. But while she is having a nap, Fausto is not. He inquires after the mysterious gentleman, and, ferreting out his identity (though the Weimarer's famous name tells him little), sends him a message. Esteemed Mr. Goethe, he writes, I'm the son of an affluent Milan banker, engaged to be married to Margherita Sozi, with whom, as I've had opportunity to hear, you have been associating lately. As I have serious intentions with the signorina myself, I ask you to communicate to me, as soon as possible, the sum which would induce you to leave her alone. With all due respect, Fausto Bosisio.*

Goethe, who has left Lake Garda in the meantime and is overtaken by the letter on his way to Brescia, reads the insulting epistle, folds it in indignation and first thinks of a duel, but is immediately steered away from this dangerous thought by his common sense. Bah, he reflects, if this had happened in my younger days, everything would have been different. Who does he think he is, this Fausto Bosisio, I'll take revenge on him and describe his odious act in my travelogue. Recollecting, however, that he would then have to disclose the background of the letter as well, he changes his mind. I'll get back at him one way or another, that Fausto, a tooth for a tooth, an eye for an eye, he wanted to buy me off, so I'll make him sell his soul instead.

The company laughs. *Brilliant*, comments Gianluca, *I'll buy you a bottle of Bardolino at the osteria over there.* They sit down to a table with a checkered spread under the restaurant pergola and order. *I haven't seen him for three months*, says an elderly lady at the next table. *I haven't seen him for three months*, Ildico takes up her cue, *so ponders the famous actress, Eleonora Duse; who knows how many liaisons he has had in the meantime, how many girls he has sweet-talked. Anyway, the poor dear must find his raison d'être in that splendid isolation of his villa, where he has been confined by the Duce because of his encroaching popularity. I burn for him still, and he knows it but ignores me. But I'm a woman, I'll use what Nature has granted me, not just my talent and curves but also my skill at pulling strings. So I've arranged a meeting with Claretta Petacci, we women know how to help each other out, she'll put in a good word for him with the Duce to release him from that golden cage at the Garda. Eleonora Duse sits down to her writing desk and pens a letter to her beloved D'Annunzio. Dearest Gabriele, I'm staying at Desenzano, barely a few kilometers from your new home, and I would like to see you and talk to you about an urgent matter. Kiss, Eleonora. Of course she doesn't forget to sprinkle the letter with the perfume that had been his gift to her.*

As has been said before, the scent which immediately evokes the author of the letter for D'Annunzio brings him no peace of mind. I can't stand women who won't accept that it's over, he thinks, straightening the black patch over his right eye. Eleonora Duse receives a written reply that he won't be at home in the afternoon. Their paths split irrevocably, for good, although they will often think of each other yet, she with bitterness, he with a bad conscience. Gabriele D'Annunzio will dedicate to her one of his most beautiful poems, but it will get lost and remain unknown to literary historians to this day.

Sad and decadent, concludes Konstantin, *But it's late and tomorrow's the final test, so let's go to bed.* As they're walking back, a couple comes toward them, with the man saying to the woman, *You've got to be careful these days, or . . . —You've got to be careful these days, or you might catch it, says Mussolini angrily to his mistress, Claretta Petacci. What were you up to last night, won't you tell me, now? Claretta sits down in an armchair in her boudoir above the salon, where Ludwig, the journalist, is still waiting for the Duce. Claretta Petacci is silent. She can't possibly tell Benito that someone has been blackmailing her over a secret from her youth. I went to see Patrizia, she answers. The truth is different, but Claretta, although she could have the blackmailer liquidated, doesn't dare to, she is afraid that her secret might leak out even sooner. I went to see Patrizia, she repeats.*

Claretta Petacci had spent the previous evenings in journalist Ludwig's company, talking to him about her lover. If she hadn't, Ludwig would have brought it all to light. Like Scheherazade, she wove story after story, unveiling the background of the great dictator whose days, at least in Ludwig's opinion, were numbered. She glossed over important facts, replacing them with no less credible fibs, some she preserved as they were, for example how the famous Eleonora Duse came asking her to intervene in the D'Annunzio affair, but at other times the threadball of her imagination rolled far from the truth and she privately wondered how Ludwig could have been taken in. Soon she began to enjoy her storytelling, she wove strands and tied them at all ends, she skipped the plot and started a story by explaining the dénouement, she conjured up digressions and tangled Ludwig in a net of figments. Before her eyes passed events which had never happened or were embellished beyond recognition, suddenly her past was just what she had always wanted it to be, and it was only at the end that she realized, exhausted with talking and drunk on fantasy, that Ludwig had helped her forget for a few evenings about the war, about domineering Benito and all the mistakes she had made. She had tasted the savor of her own story.

Aleksandar falls silent, the others are silent, too, and Gianluca nods. *Yes, savory stories*, he says. Bjørn clears his throat, breaking the universal contemplation. *Well, now tell us how those three stories really ended*, Almut challenges Gainluca, but he simply smirks, glancing toward the lake mischievously. *I made them up*, he says.

The participants have arrived at the door of the pension where they're staying. Saying goodbye, Gianluca heads for home. *Tomorrow, after the test*, he thinks, *I'll invite them for a limoncello and ask them about three stories they consider best in the world.*

Patterns of the World

MY NAME IS GRETA Poppenheim, Greta first name, Poppenheim last name, and I like to watch the full moon-Luna. If you look at it very closely through binoculars, you can spot tiny discolored dots-blotches and it seems-appears-looks like embroidered lace. Lace is like patterns of our world reflected on a distant planet, I can imagine on its surface the lace profile-contours of a woman, a delicately crafted flower wreath, or a doily of symmetrical patterns.

I visit a doctor by the name of Josef Breuer, Josef first name, Breuer last. Years ago, there was always a lady-girl waiting for her turn in the anteroom to his office. She grasped that I was never in a hurry and we had a chat sometimes. Her name was Marta, that's a first name not a last, not a last name, and she was blind but not from the start-birth, she'd only gone blind a couple of years before, and even though she had problems-complaints of her own, she knew at once what was wrong with me. *You talk so funny*, she said at our third meeting, *It's like my writing*, she said, *when they read my writing to me, I can't believe I've written that, Mama once read out for me a letter I'd composed the day before.* In a way that letter had been like my speech, she said-opined, she was inserting smaller boxes into larger ones, and when the last was crammed full, she'd start from scratch with the largest. Unable to see what she'd written and sometimes unable to recall her thoughts, try as she might, she would repeat the same in a variety of ways. I too sometimes use one and the same box to say-express different things. Or the-other-way-round-vice-versa.

Marta definitely couldn't have played the "you tell me" game with the doctor because she can't-see-is-blind, but I could. He showed me a picture-image, and I had to tell what was represented, always in different words. Once he showed me the picture of a big oak tree on a hill in the rain, with a rainbow in the background. I said: *Rainbow and oak on a hill in rain.* And he said: *Romantic fall.* Then it was my turn again. I said: *Oak and rainbow on a slope with rain,* and he: *Rainbow tree.* Me again: *Oak, rainbow, hill, rain,* and he: *Rainy hill.* In my opinion he didn't include-cover everything, though he protested that he'd been the more creative one. *But such creativity-invention doesn't match the truth,* I answered-countered, while he mumbled something about assembled speech.

Mama revealed-disclosed to me once, when I prodded her, that I'd struck my head against a stone when I fell off my bike. It was then that I partly lost the faculty of speech and had to be taught again. I learned faster than little children, fortunately-luckily-thank-God, but then I was able to learn from ready-made patterns. If the Professor said: *Today is a fine sunny day,* I could replace sunny with cloudy, day with evening, and-so-on-and-so-forth, I can say *Tomorrow was an ugly sunny evening, Yesterday was a fine rainy night,* varying the sentence elements as I please, so rich is language, so many facets has the world. If someone says *I'm going to the store,* I can say *I'm going to the drawer* though I've never heard it said. This is what the Professor calls deduction, adding that I wasn't born with it, the Professor knows a lot, much more than I do even if my head is full of formulas which are my patterns of the world.

I meet the Professor once every-two-weeks-a-fortnight and we discuss lots of things. Supposedly-allegedly he even hypnotized me once. After each visit-session the Professor dictates to the nurse-aide, and she writes while he uses such expressions as language universals, language competence, transformation rules. I keep quiet-still in the meantime, listening and trying to memorize, these words might come in handy some time. Once he suggested that I should start learning French but then changed his mind, he said that it was too early, that I should first "learn the deeper structures of my language and become more creative"-inventive. *The French*, he said, *have other language patterns.*

When I'm well, I make bobbin lace, which is the most fascinating thing in the world. I never make two identical pieces, not even for my twin nephews, though it makes them bicker-quarrel. I collect lace too, I've countless-innumerable pieces, the finest are the lace profile-contours of a woman, a delicately crafted flower wreath, and a doily of symmetrical patterns. My favorite, though, is a piece of lace formed like the Gulf of Trieste with hinterland, I made it myself but the memory of those days is bitter. The most beautiful samples in my collection are Italian and Flanders laces from the sixteenth and seventeenth centuries.

My name is Greta Poppenheim, and when the moon-Luna is full, I go out of myself, that's what the doctor calls it. He says that I'm hysterical and that he has acquainted with my case the famous-renowned doctor Sigmund, can't remember if that's his first or last name. When the moon-Luna is full, I don't feel like eating or drinking, I grow very sad-melancholy and don't even want to live, I feel as if I'm sinking down a chimney. This is simply something that happens every month-moon, simply part and parcel of my usual disorder. When it's happening to me, I feel terribly-dreadfully distressed, I feel as if I want to say-tell something in a language that doesn't exist, in a language that only I know, that-is-to-say-I-mean, one that I used to know before I struck my head against that stone.

One reason for this feeling must-may be that in such crisis moments, as Doctor Breuer calls them, I find myself bereft of voice. Aphonia, that's his technical term for it. At such times I just gasp for air, casting about for non-existent words, tossing like a fish out of water, and nobody understands my distress. At such-these times my consciousness seems to lag behind the real events, I seem to follow the events around me with a time lag.

As the doctor tells me, it has been scientifically proved by his colleagues that we humans become aware of our decision half-a-zero-point-five seconds after it's been formed in the brain. Breuer doesn't agree-hold with this view because, as he says, it would mean that there's no free will at all, but for my part I'd be relieved if it were true. That would mean that what happens to me isn't my fault, that I'm merely a mute observer of this world, an observer who speaks up only when she has found what she thinks-believes is the most suitable word.

I've read in a magazine that people can be grouped into several types, there were drawings of them as well, all furnished with descriptions of the psyche and physique belonging to each physical type. It soothes me, this certainty that people can be sorted into compartments, just like the clothes I fold and store in the wardrobe. I wonder, though, which group I belong to or if there is some outside group for me. I couldn't place Tobias either, he's such an extraordinary person. I met him in 1883 in Trieste, where Dad-Papa took me on holiday-leave to breathe fresh air and forget my problems-complaints.

Tobias Hohenlohe, Tobias first name, Hohenlohe last, is a cousin of the Trieste governor, the Imperial and Royal Deputy Conrad, of whom the irredentists have little good to say because he's convinced-believes that Trieste should be a multinational city. Dad-Papa and me were their guests at their house, and Tobias, too, came every day to visit his relative. Being of the same age-years we were drawn closer and closer, we would go for walks and sometimes to his office too. Tobias is a cartographer, he has to revise the maps of Trieste and its surroundings, rewrite the names of the surrounding-places-nearby-toponyms in German. He said he had to provide a truer-more-real picture of the world. Maps consist of letters and images, he said-explained to me, but I was reminded at once of patterned lace. He showed-displayed for me old portolan charts and maps of the African continent, their blank spots covered with mythological figures, fantastic animals, and exotic plants, for-because a map should have no empty spaces. We both daydreamed over those fantastic lines and jagged color splotches written over with minute toponyms, riddled with parallels and meridians. With maps you can refurbish history, erase borders and draw new ones, the map is your head in which you can give things your own, different names, it's the writing of a novel and the making of new lace, it's the dream of reality in the reality of a dream. The Trieste *Bora* drove us along the coast like two sailboats, puffing out my skirt and trying to wrench away my sunshade while Tobias pointed his finger at distant-faraway points on the sea, telling stories of unknown places. He escorted me to Trieste antique shops, bric-à-brac shops, and flea markets, where I bought-purchased some beautiful samples of bobbin lace. Once our hands touched, by chance-accident, our fingers intertwining above the unknown landscapes drawn on fine paper. But here, on the Austro-Hungarian-Italian border, the reverie was cut short.

In that late spring of 1883 I fell in love with Tobias Hohenlohe but he soon began to evade me. At-first-at-the-start he did show an interest in me, or so I imagine, but when he saw-perceived my disorder, he shut himself in his own world of geographic iconography, walled off by a front of courteous yet cool politeness. He soared above the landscape like a bird, and all I was to him was the cut-off curve of a sinking river in the fields below. On our last walk through Barcola I touched on my forebodings: *Why does your hand seem to withdraw a little when I try to touch it? Why does your hand appear to recoil when I want to draw near? I have the feeling that your hand, when I reach for it, moves away a little; why? Why do you almost imperceptibly pull your hand away when I want to move mine closer? Why?*

The answer I already knew-saw.

In high summer the heat overpowered Father, who had left

Vienna practically for the first time in his life, and we set-out-headed for home. When I realized that the chink of hope had closed and that I was left alone again, like Atlas carrying the weight of the world on his shoulders, I had to live through yet another day with no voice. With no man, no starting point-meridian to lean on, none to confide to that my thoughts were like cakes which can be baked in the same pan over and over again.

I've started therapy with Doctor Breuer again. Since that summer I've sunk down the chimney several times. It's all the fault of the stone that may have crumbled from its mold in the moon-lunar crater, dropping just on the spot where I was to fall and hit it. This is all, nothing more. I must not cross the line-boundary. All I know is that my name is Greta Poppenheim, Greta first name, Poppenheim last, and when I say that, I say all the things I'm not.

Cyrano

How little of Marta has been left for me: Zeus and that empty cognac bottle in our "pleasure cabinet." I can't toss it away, we emptied it together and now it's there, an empty but not mute piece of evidence, its emptiness testifying to its one-time fullness, just as my widowerhood is proof that I was married once.

That's the way it goes, dear Counselor, one needs something to fill one's pallid, lukewarm days, so I never hesitated when I saw the announcement but joined the Mask theater group the very next day. The director, a good-natured and, as befits good nature, chubby fellow, a widower himself, gave me the leading role right after the audition, casting me as Cyrano de Bergerac. As you certainly know, Miss Counselor, Cyrano is in love with his cousin Roxane, who was played by . . . let me just call her Roxane to avoid profaning her name needlessly. And now you will have guessed what I wanted to tell you, dear Counselor, I'm writing to your magazine column in the hopes of being comforted by a wise word or a bit of advice, though the highest absurdity is that I used to be a counselor myself, not in a magazine like you but on the radio. Nobody close to me knows it, but on the air I used to introduce myself as Doctor C. I had calls coming in from all kinds of people, one had marriage trouble, another couldn't sleep at night for jealousy, the third had bouts of depression, the fourth had been vainly searching all his life for a kindred soul. I answered as best I knew how, I'm no trained psychologist but I've always been told that I was good at giving comfort, and when a friend, an owner of that radio channel, invited me to join, I didn't refuse his offer.

In short, I fell passionately in love with her, my fellow actress Roxane, on my way to the theater I would quiver with excitement, my heart pounding like crazy. But she had been married for a dozen years and had a child to boot. And, worst of all, she knew nothing of my inner struggles. She was always very kind to me and when we went for a drink after the rehearsal, she often sat down next to me to talk about her private affairs as well, about her son, about her feeble mother, who she refused to pack off to a home, about all the places she had traveled with her husband, about her current reading, but there was never a hint at any feeling deeper than friendship. As I said, my legs used to wobble on approaching the theater, but as we stood together on the stage, all tension slackened, I felt calm and strong, and this feeling lasted to the end of the rehearsal, when—more's the pity—I slipped back into my own wretched skin. It's not as if the character I played was a self-confident charmer, by no means, I represented a musketeer who is brave, an excellent fencer and a brilliant rhymer. *He who has seen her smile has known perfection*, he says. *Instilling into trifles grace's essence, / Divinity in every careless gesture.*[1] But Cyrano is hampered by his big nose, which makes him so ugly that he never dares to hope for requited love. *Come now, bethink you! . . . The fond hope to be / Beloved, e'en by some poor graceless lady, / Is, by this nose of mine, for aye bereft me; / —This lengthy nose which, go where'er I will, / Pokes yet a quarter-mile ahead of me; / But I may love—and who? 'Tis Fate's decree / I love the fairest—how were't otherwise?* But why am I even rehashing this for you, Miss Counselor—or should I simply call you *colleague?*—you certainly know the story, I just wanted to say that I, too, feel like a dauntless hero when I'm on stage,

---

1   The English translations of the passages from Edmond Rostand's play *Cyrano de Bergerac* are taken from the Project Gutenberg e-book of Cyrano de Bergerac, http://www.gutenberg.org/files/1254/1254-h/1254-h. htm. (Translator's note.)

but behind the scenes I shrink back into a commonplace bore. Except that my face isn't disfigured by a large and ugly nose, my flaw is elsewhere, my problem is Marta, she is my handicap.

What are you doing to me? I heard her speak up from a cloud, her voice spilling down together with the sunrays, the kind you see in Baroque church paintings, What are you doing to me, don't you see that I can't stand up for myself. Should I come down and box your ears, should I go to her and tell her what a chicken you are, should I hug you to remind you of the good times we had, what should I do? So Marta talked to me day and night after each rehearsal and the only thing she never said was, It's only right that you should be enjoying life even after my death, the heart can't be commanded anyway. Marta is my guilty conscience, she holds me back, but frankly, dear Counselor, I couldn't have declared my love to Roxane directly, not at my age, a freshman can afford to fail an exam but a senior finds it embarrassing.

I was very fond of Marta, we married for love. We couldn't have children but enjoyed instead the company of Zeus, our German shepherd, and our many friends who often visited us. I can say that we were happy, not downright bursting with happiness but happy in a contented, complacent way. When I realized I was in love with Roxane, I pondered the light this love cast on my marriage and discovered that my love for Marta had been one thing while my love for Roxane was something completely different, that those were two loves. Marta would never have understood, neither would Roxane, perhaps, if she had known what I felt.

And so every wayward thought of Roxane sent Marta shaking her finger at me from the clouds and thundering hollowly, You can't possibly do such a thing to me, I'm powerless, don't you understand?—No, I don't understand, Marta, your powerlessness is your power, I would have liked to scream up at her, what did you go and do *that* for . . . Do you think you made it easy for me? At first I racked my brains why you'd done it at all, then I was crushed by the terrible burden of guilt because I hadn't been able to dissuade you, but how could I when I had no idea that you were capable of such an act. And at last I grasped that the main point of the whole thing was my defeat. Is that what you wanted, Marta? Prove that I'd failed flat on my face? I mean . . . downing all the bottles from our pleasure cabinet and stuffing yourself with all kinds of pills, that's what I call plain irresponsibility. Irresponsibility to you, to me, didn't you ever think of me? Or did you strike out on purpose . . .

I apologize, dear Counselor, I got carried away, but do tell me how I could love another woman, even if silently, invisibly, when I can't tell if I'm still bound to the first. What binds me to Marta is a sense of alliance, a shared marital guilt but then unfinished love as well, love as a habit broken by her betrayal, I don't really know, for me it's treachery if everything looks dandy and then one day, zap, she drops dead of her own free will. What am I supposed to think? Darling, I've gone on a long trip, never to come back, or: You wretch, didn't you see how unhappy I was, couldn't you keep me alive? You can't even begin to imagine how miserable I was those first months after her death. I just cried and cried, there was no stopping me. And now you're going to ask me, like a proper counselor, what reasons she might have had for taking her own life. I don't know, maybe just sheer disgust with everything, sheer listlessness and indifference, depression almost, because that's what she was like in that last year, maybe she gave up on me but I never saw it in my blindness, so that I'm still wondering today where I screwed up. All of this came as a huge, painful surprise. Oh, Marta, if I'd known that text before, I'd have quoted at you Cyrano's words about autumn leaves: *Ay, see how brave they fall, / In their last journey downward from the bough, / To rot within the clay; yet, lovely still, / Hiding the horror of the last decay, / With all the wayward grace of careless flight!*

Well, as you know, dear Counselor, our heroic comedy has Roxane fall in love with Christian, handsome but without

Cyrano's knack for poetry, which happens to be high in Roxane's good books. Cyrano, on the other hand, has the gift of words, but he is ugly. In short, the one with bread has no teeth and the one with teeth has no bread. And so they hit on a scheme to complement each other's gifts: Cyrano will compose rhymes and whisper them in darkness to handsome Christian, Christian will recite them under Roxane's balcony, and together they will create the perfect man.

One half of my perfect man was the stage musketeer while the other half spent his Saturdays in the studio, doling out advice to frustrated housewives, pimply young men, and dreamy damsels over thirty. There I was flooded by the same feeling as at the theater, I was someone else, a hero saving lives, a Superman whizzing through the air to offer a hanky to a girl crying in the park, a Robin Hood bubbling with empathy and sympathy. And a sorry sight picking my way home in the streetlamp glow. I could no longer bear the contrast between the hangdog and the great hero, it was tearing me apart, and being the introvert type, I opted for just one half of the perfect man, the radio half, for there I was concealed and only my voice was heard, while the musketeer half should withdraw, being out of place. At least I'll know that I'm suffering because Roxane is in my heart rather than in my sight, I said to myself; after all, what made the real Cyrano unhappy was not love but looks. I fed the director some bull about being ill and he patted me reassuringly on the back without asking more questions, Never mind, Peter can stand in, he said. I was sad and surprised by my own strength at leaving her. I didn't say goodbye personally, I couldn't pluck up the courage, but I did write a letter, letting her know that I was not indifferent. *In fairy tales / When to the ill-starred Prince the lady says / "I love you!" all his ugliness fades fast— / But I remain the same, up to the last,* I quoted Cyrano, who comes, mortally wounded, to say farewell to Roxane, disclosing that those bewitching verses and letters were not penned by her Prince Charming but by himself.

I shook hands with the director and some fellow actors,

leaving my letter for Roxane in the changing room. Trudging down the washed-out pavement, with my sorry figure reflected in its dark asphalt mirror, I could feel Marta shaking her head and sighing as a mother sighs over an unruly child, sighing so hard that a chilling breeze breathed from the dark cumulus clouds. You can just shut up, I snapped, if you hadn't sneaked off behind my back, I wouldn't have to seek love elsewhere.

You're wondering, What does the guy want from me, Miss Professional Counselor—well, you have a psychology degree and I'm calling on you to tell me how you see my situation. Two months passed since my farewell to the theater and then, three weeks ago, a new caller is put through at the studio, I freeze on hearing her voice. Good evening, Dr. C, this is Roxane speaking, she introduces herself, fancying how brilliantly she has concealed herself behind a theater pseudonym. I have a problem, she tells me. I didn't believe I would be able to answer at all, all that was wrung from my throat was a hoarse hello, but luckily she noticed nothing and continued. I've fallen in love, I've only realized now that I love someone, a person who has been near me all this time but I never noticed him, and now he's left my life and I haven't known till now that I love him, she said. Then she paused and I was expected to say something comforting. I had never been in such dire straits. But then I had a brainwave and replied in a velvety voice, such as I'd rarely succeeded in coaxing out of my throat, Ah, Roxane, would you happen to know the unhappy love story of your namesake and her cousin Cyrano, it's like yours, Rostand's Roxane didn't know either that she loved the big-nosed musketeer till it was too late, only then did she realize that he'd been burning for her all the time and that it was he who had written those marvelous verses. There was a moment's silence at the other end of the line, broken by a rattle. Yes, I know the story, she said uncertainly. Her shyness filled me with new courage. *I go in your shadow; / Let me be wit for you, be you my beauty*, says the protagonist to Christian, remember? What about you, Roxane, that's my question for you, do you love with your eyes or your heart? More silence at the other end. I must admit, she says after a few seconds, that I barely noticed him before, he's very inconspicuous, I certainly wouldn't have fallen for his looks, well, he's not particularly handsome but not ugly either . . . I refused to be confounded. *What if he be a lout unskilled?* Cyrano asks Roxane when she tells him of her love for Christian, but she counters: *No, his bright locks, like D'Urfé's heroes . . .* What a rum lot you ladies are, I patronized her, careful not to lose my mellow tone. We women fall in love with both the inner and the outer man, she ventured, I even heard of a radio listener who fell in love with a reporter's voice and found and married him, some woman might fall in love with your voice, too . . . What "some woman," I thought to myself, when all I want is you . . . *Ay, and let me die to-day, / Since, all unconscious, she mourns me—in him*, I recalled de Bergerac's words at Christian's death. I was my own Christian, hiding behind musketeer roles and radio waves, and the Cyranoesque, bulbous nose was embodied in Marta. A prime mess.

I don't know how to tell him that I've only recognized now what a wonderful man he is, his letter was the most enchanting thing I've ever read, continued ethereal Roxane, should I write back, call, visit, what should I do . . . because I'm married, she added in a lower voice. Listen to your heart, listen to your heart, I almost sang in an exaggeratedly blasé tone, And now, music! I pressed the green button, heaving a sigh of relief.

What happened afterward, dear Counselor, caught and whirled me headlong into the jaws of doom. That very evening I quit my job on the radio, that is to say, abandoned the second half of my Superman, and returned the next day to the theater to reclaim the first. Explaining to the director that my health had miraculously improved, I asked if there might be another role for me. Of course, he replied, we're going to stage Pirandello's *Mixing it Up*, the first reading's on Friday. I spent the week in a tremor of anticipation.

On Friday, the reading rehearsal was attended by all of us but Roxane. She had lost her head over an engineer, a widower who had lived for years in the house across the street. It was just before he moved out that he finally sent her a letter, and she fell for him, left her husband, dragged off her kid, too, and went to live with her new lover, so I was told by a fellow actor, a retired public servant.

Life is one single, huge misunderstanding, dear Counselor, Roxane unwittingly loves Cyrano but runs after Christian because she thinks that he is the one she loves, I'm running after a woman who never looked at me but who had, so I believed, finally come to love me, she herself realizes that she loves a man she hasn't even noticed in years, and to cap it all, Marta's not done with me yet or I with Marta. *What say you*, dear Counselor, *It is useless? Ay, I know, / But who fights ever hoping for success? / I fought for lost cause, and for fruitless quest!*

Comet Hunting

NIGHT IS FALLING, MY time is coming, my shape changing into a werewolf, the organ booming, the oboe trumpeting into the dusk which is taking its leave in the west, with tones of yellow azure shading into black. The here recedes from the beyond, which is about to flood the world with all its omnipotence for a total of eleven hours and three minutes.

Master Wilhelm, Master Wilhelm, I hear my housekeeper's voice, *supper is ready,* my dear Mitzy, what about the food of the gods, think I to myself, who am I to be granted all this?

Master Wilhelm, says Mitzy, *a letter has come,* handing it to me above the steam swirling from the tureen. I break the Royal Society seal, skim through the text . . . *reason to infer that it might be something else . . . the body moves too fast . . .* etcetera, etcetera, etcetera, it was such doubts that the letter voiced. What the hell . . .?

I ate up hurriedly, *Call Caroline,* I ordered Mitzy, leaving for my little observatory. The spangled sky had been obscured by clouds, no observation tonight, the night would be spent grinding and polishing my lenses.

I had barely drawn the plan for a new lens and finished its description when Caroline appeared. *Come, little sister, I must show you something,* I told her, and all out of breath she took up the letter, with her eyes darting across the paper, finally pausing, lifting, and looking at me quizzically. *What is this about?* she asked. *That you've been mistaken? That it's not a comet but something else?*

In point of fact, the very night after the publication of my letter to the Royal Society had sent many European astronomers calculating the elements of the elongated ellipse in which the body of my discovery was assumed to move. *Account of a comet* was how I headed my letter to the royal observatory, only to receive now the reply that it was most likely not a comet at all. *The body moves too fast.* What the hell . . .?

Don't swear, said Caroline, *God can overhear you now that you're so close to the stars.*

To the stars, not to Heaven, I corrected her, *the stars are but God's trinkets.*

No, said Caroline, *the stars are His creation.*

Hurrying to the octagonal chapel the next morning, I overheard Mitzy wailing about the master never sleeping anymore, just staring through those telescopes or polishing lenses by night, playing the organ in the church or the oboe in the orchestra by day, and it struck me that my own body, too, was moving too fast. The thought that it might be but a mirror image of the heavenly body I dismissed at once as bold and conceited. I had never believed in old astrological prattle either, although I'm persuaded that mine is not a profiteering mercurial character but largely a saturnine one, melancholic, solitary, artistic. I had, after all, composed quite a few symphonies, which are now and then even performed for the public. Besides, I'm bound to the contemplation of heaven, nothing to match it, though I feel alive only writing my music. Staring into heaven, I'm paralyzed by fear. Torn between heaven and music, poor soul, not even Caroline can understand me. For her, nothing exists but God and Heaven, she took her punishment, her typhoid fever at ten leaving her no taller than four feet as if it were her fate, she has remained small before God while I dare to stand on tiptoe and poke into God's abode.

Surely the booming of the church organ must reach to the eternal vault above. The pastor was looking at me askance as if to say, *Is it not enough to play for the Supreme Creator, why pore at night over material evidence for His existence?* Well, and what of all this luxury, I retorted in my head, all these Gothic arches and stained glass, come to my observatory, it's all brick, my shrine, and yet I reach the stars from it.

After Mass I hurried to the orchestra practice. I was out of breath, the oboe resisted me, what wretched drudgery, this practice, every single day, at least the stars are asleep at the time so I only miss them during the concerts, I told myself. Waiting in front of the concert hall was Caroline, with two more letters in hand, *The first is by Hornsby, the other from Greenwich,* she told me. *I cannot see the newly discovered body at all,* stated the former, while Maskelayne, according to the latter, had in fact noticed it but couldn't measure its apparent motion among the stars. The stars in Maskelayne's telescope were too faint and smudged to observe except with the ocular entirely darkened, for they vanished as soon as the cross-hair reticle was lit up to measure their movements.

No one had an instrument to match mine. The wooden scaffold looming sixty-six feet high embraced a giant telescope, ten feet in length and a diameter of eighteen and a half inches; I had cast and manufactured its two hundred specular mirrors myself. Naturally I'm proud of it, but what matters is that Heaven is my religion, my awe, my stupefaction. All I have to boast of is my piety, for I've gazed into space more than any man before me.

In my time, comet hunting was all the rage. Everyone wanted a comet of his own, to have his name nailed to the sky for all eternity. Hornsby swiping at heaven with his butterfly net, Maskelayne shooting his rifle at starkind, all of Europe blinking upward, stretching up their palms and trying to beat the stars from heaven like ripe pears. Europe on stilts, aspiring to heavenly glory. None but Caroline knew how to remain a midget while serving the solar system. *Close to the gamma star!* she would call to me when I was searching for some nebula, helping me, directing me with the aid of charts, *Toward Sagittarius! In that constellation!* as I goggled through the telescope. Her devotion was different from mine. Her devotion burned like love, mine was a duty to the Higher Power, she would have done everything for God from her heart, I would have done so from awe, an obligation to serve the System. She was the ant, sacrificing herself for the giant out of love, I was the crumb, observing the universe in amazement. That was why I came to suppress my true love, abandoning and subordinating music to what I deemed more "right."

All those galaxies, nebulae, milky ways, and Saturn's rings circling above my head, all that is given, breathtaking as it may be, while the music comes from somewhere between my chest and stomach, heaving forth and bursting into freedom. The feeling is indescribable, miles away from the systematic recording of the sky. Even if music, too, is mathematics, swelling by rules of its own.

I can't see the newly discovered body at all, Hornsby had written. Caroline smirked. You blind bat, I thought, why not sleep at night rather than look up into the dark, your insomnia is mere ambition, while mine is . . . Yes, my insomnia is wakefulness in the presence of All, the One, the Supreme, there's an imp that won't let me catch a wink, nudging me when my eyelids are already dropping over my eyeballs, grinning *No dozing, there are far weightier matters in store for you.*

The next Monday morning was shrouded in a thick milky fog that struck me as unreal, but I put that down to having slept only two hours. Under my window I heard the clatter of hooves, the screech of wooden wheels halting in front of our house, the whinny of horses. Mitzy came running up the stairs. *Master Wilhelm, Master Wilhelm*, she panted, *he's come, my God, he's here* . . . As she was still struggling for breath, I drew the curtain aside and saw a page opening the door of a carriage. A moment later there emerged a man in an ermine cloak, with golden linen garments glittering underneath and a light gray curled wig on his head . . . George, George III!

Drained of all strength, Mitzy slumped down on the bench in my cabinet, and as I reached the first floor, Caroline was feverishly trotting to and fro, adjusting her dress, dusting random pieces of furniture with her hands, biting her lip and muttering to herself.

There was a sharp knock, I no longer remember how it happened, or what, but suddenly I was in my hall, bowing to His Majesty, who was awkwardly standing on my doorstep between two escorts, whistling an Händel air in embarrassment.

Here my memory blacks out again, and the next scene I recall is the King sitting in my "astronomical" armchair and talking to me. To me, poor little Wilhelm. *Mr. Herschel*, he says, *your comet is no comet, your comet is a planet*, he says, winding around his finger a strand of the wool used by Mitzy to knit my scarf, making the ball prance merrily on the carpet. I almost burst out laughing, what is this ignoramus of a king babbling about. *Your Majesty, no new planet has been discovered since antiquity*, I tell him humbly, but he smiles at me, confident and secure, as if he knew more about astronomy than anyone in the world. *It has been confirmed by the Astronomer Royal Maskelayne*, he went on, *others are jostling for new comets, but you have discovered a planet. I have already suggested to the Greenwich Observatory the name Herschel.*

I felt like laughing, not for joy but for the absurdity of it. Who was I that I should be destined to discover a new planet? This had to be another bout of George III's insanity, which was the talk of the country by that time. The King was said to suffer from occasional attacks of dementia—one time he had reputedly interrupted a solemn concert, another time he had pursued the chambermaids—and they said it might be an inherited disorder, porphyria. As if to prove his insanity, His Majesty snaps the wool strand, bends over to pick up the ball of wool, and tosses it high in the air, making the skein strike the ceiling and bounce back into his hands. *A planet, I tell you, it was confirmed by telescopes modeled on yours, yours is best*, he tells me as if he were my colleague. Embarrassed, Caroline is looking at the floor.

Why has the King traveled from London to the country just to tell me the news? *I'm offering you an opportunity to escape from the orchestra, move to the capital, and devote yourself to astronomy alone, for which I will pay you an annuity of two hundred pounds,* he says. My head spins. I would no longer have to serve in the orchestra or play the church organ, that's fine with me, but I should give up composing as well. He tells me that my compositions are considered of little worth anyway, and besides, freedom from cares never produces high art. *True art is born in poverty,* he remarks sagely. Rising from the armchair, he saunters around the room, picks an apple from the basket on the commode, and starts juggling the apple in one hand and the skein in the other. A court fool rather than a king, I reflect.

I should, then, devote myself to astronomy alone, suppressing the artist in me and choosing the all-powerful universe over my microcosm. *The world is ruled by the universe, not by human creations,* resumes the ruler of this world while tossing the two little rounded satellites.

What would the stars do without us, I venture, *who would observe them?*

The stars are only for the elect, replies the mad king, going on to suggest the maddest exchange in the world.

Above all, I am offering you a once-in-a-lifetime experience, he says, *you will be King for a week, and I will be Herschel in the meantime.* I burst out laughing, which I shouldn't have done in front of His Majesty, but still. Even Caroline, who stood leaning against the fireplace, smiled.

After moments of silence, I agreed. Agreed to be as mad as the King.

It was the oddest week of my life. Of course we never attempted to keep the exchange secret: everyone close to us was told that we, ruler and subject, would swap roles in the ancient carnival tradition, but with no occasional change of clothing.

During that week I learned that the King ruled by clever bribery and that he had allies in his ministers, particularly Bute and North. It was the first time I took up the scepter, the first time I sat down on the throne, the first time I had a royal dinner, the first time I spoke the royal language. The Queen kept her distance.

The fifth day was the worst. Having requested an audience, North came to tell me that the American colonies were rebelling. This was a worse problem than the Irish question or the Roman Catholics' rights, which I managed to play by ear. But the colonies . . . The rebellion should be crushed by force, North demanded.

Really, who was I, a speck of dust in space, to make decisions about a military intervention and the life of natives on another continent? The insomnia which plagued me those days was quite different from that caused by the all-powerful cosmos. Now, George III had set the rule that I was not to consult him during that week and that he was to leave me alone as well. I had exchanged heavenly observation for earthly rule, and I realized that I felt incomparably lighter when face-to-face with the universe.

And what was the King up to in the meantime?

Me? I was plagued by insomnia, too. I sauntered around the observatory, watching the sky through various telescopes. On cloudy nights I would examine the lenses and arcane plans explained to me by Caroline, eat Mitzy's stews, and feel my greatness. I sent a letter to the Greenwich Royal Observatory, proposing that the new planet should be named Georgium Sidus,

George's Star. No comet-hunting for me as for those other pygmies: I had landed a planet. I was Herschel, Wilhelm Herschel, who was to discover over ten thousand nebulae and star clusters and the satellites of the new planet, and to be awarded a medal for his achievements in science. I was the lord of Earth and Sky. At full moon I didn't take the shape of a werewolf but turned into Master Wilhelm, the organ booming, the oboe trumpeting into the dusk taking its leave in the west, with tones of yellow azure shading into black, the here and the beyond intertwined.

And it was as many as thirty years after My Majesty died, turning into a meager comet after all, that someone suggested the name Uranus for the new planet.

Aegeus

EVEN SUNDAYS ARE NOT what they once were—gloomy, I mean—people swarm around the shops, which are of course open, and have forgotten about contemplation, about the spiritual. Oh Filip, my Filip, walking along the old coast path today I bumped into the custodian of the Coastal Gallery and he said that the exhibition will take place. How pleased I was, but to tell you the truth I'm also a little scared: if it happens so quickly, I thought, then my final goal will soon be fulfilled and I'll have no more reason to live. Then this young art historian tells me that he needs to look through a lot more material, that the gallery program is fixed for some time ahead and that the exhibition will take place only in November of next year. I was so relieved, Filip, don't be offended, but I said to him, *oh dear, not until November next year, what if I don't survive that long? You will, of course you will*, he said, *you have to—now you have a reason to live at least until then.* As if he had read my thoughts; it did me good, though I shook my head.

Thus we jump from one goal to another: these goals make our lives scan, like hurdles in a horse race. For me, the highest and widest hurdle was your confinement. At the time I said to myself that I had to survive the war only to see you at least once more—that's what I lived for. And when that was achieved I set myself a new task: you know which, it's as painful for me to talk about as it was for you to think about Pino. This hurdle that I couldn't get over I call a blind fence. As if I had to jump over a pole and at the last moment the groom removed it. Here we go again with banal philosophizing, saying that a person can't have everything.

And it was of Pino that I thought during my Sunday walk, when the waves foamed and splashed the cracked asphalt. It wasn't your fault—get that out of your head—Pino went of his own accord. But he was like you, challenging both natural and supernatural forces. *As if he wanted to challenge life itself and to cross the line, to risk being swallowed by the dark unknown somewhere beyond safety, which most of us fear like death*, is what it said in the Biennale catalog in 1970. Do you remember?

I don't know if the dead remember: it would be nice if they did, if it wasn't only the living who were tormented by the past; when we are, it means that we're no longer jumping over hurdles, not even blind ones. But I have one more goal in front of me: your exhibition, your last present to me, for which I thank you, Filip. You'll get precious little from it, only posthumous fame, and I don't know if that means much to you. You were always above all that: you said they didn't understand you and that they wouldn't even after your death, as if in the end you didn't really care. Do you remember that charcoal drawing that you called Evolution, with five human figures, gradually aging, the first a child and so on, the seventy-year-old still quite dignified, but the last, the centenarian, looked like a Neanderthal. Evolution in the wrong direction. And then that critic who misinterpreted it all— you didn't have much luck with the critics. But the young man I met today filled me with hope, especially regarding the care that he will devote to you and the time he will take. November next year!

It was very windy today, the first chilly September *Bora* was cutting like a knife, and I thought of that time in Dalmatia when we were angry with the whole world and went on holiday in October instead of August. And it was somehow dead, yes, the dead holidays, we called it later. Not a soul around, just some sullen locals, the *Tramontana* and sour wine. But a number of good canvases resulted that sold for a tidy sum. And the very next year you didn't paint the sea anymore. Yes, because of him. He sailed off in just such a tempest, like the storm on that Dalmatian painting. I loved him like he was my own son, in time even more, because you wouldn't have children with me. That was the punishment for Pino's death: don't tell me that you simply couldn't have any more offspring because it would have been a kind of betrayal of Pino. I paid for your stormy enchantment with risk; it bound the two of you together more than anything.

Oh, Filip, will I live to see next November? The retrospective is intended to exhibit the best canvases, even though they will be hard to gather together. Some have been sold, some given away, thirteen of them are at home and two very good ones are at Lucija's house. I never really understood why you married her: she was too ordinary for you, too predictable. Lucija is like a mist, you said, drifting around slow and gray. So I wanted to be that much different; at the beginning I was scared to death that you would leave me. And at first, I admit, I was jealous of Pino, but of Lucija never. Of course, I only saw her three times, the last when she brought Pino a birthday present. Ha, that birthday, it seemed more like yours than his: you invited more of your friends than he did his schoolmates. *This is my Pino,* you shouted, when you were really topped up, *look at him, my masterpiece!* At the time your riotous behavior didn't embarrass me, on the contrary, I joined in, I liked your bohemian nature, I wanted to be like that too—me, the unfulfilled artist who contented herself teaching fine art, I replaced my "ordinariness" with your "differentness," that's what I said to myself, I impregnated myself with it, otherwise I wouldn't have survived, I loved you so much, I still do: you were my guide, my Picasso, the son I never had. You were everything. So in spite of everything I was able to accept Pino that easily: he was joined to you, he was the blood that ran through your veins. During the marvelous revelry at our home you went to wake him and in front of your friends you stood him, all sleepy and blinking in the sharp light, on the rotating base for models. *This is my son, look what a Paris he is!* He stood there, poor thing, a boyish figure, a gummy-eyed Greek *kouros* in pajamas, and he didn't know what to do with himself. A good thing that Lucija died before him—you didn't have that good fortune.

A posthumous retrospective, that's how the young custodian of the Coastal Gallery that I met on my walk today referred to the exhibition. It sounds awful: posthumous. I can already see what the opening will be like: first a short speech by a local art critic, then a few words over a glass or two with friends and acquaintances. But a celebration without the one being celebrated is sad, like a wake. Do you remember Pino's wake? So many friends had never gathered before. Actually, in the end it turned into quite a party, at which you of course sparkled when you drank some bottles of red almost at one go. *The air is hot, the sky is cloudy, the earth silent, the sea murky, you boomed like a tragic actor, and the sailors steer their laden boats into the harbor before the storm*, Sirk replied, *lonely white sails in the murky distance*, you rumbled in response like Triton, *rudderless she sails and without anchor across the waves*, each mumbled to themselves the ending of Murn's poem.

No poem suited him more—rudderless and without anchor. He forced his way into danger, shipwreck, self-destruction. I never told you that I caught him at the age of fifteen swigging turps left in a bottle in your studio. No, he hadn't made a mistake, he knew it was poisonous. I immediately called an ambulance; the doctor yelled at me, *Madam, are you completely mad, your son . . . He's not my son*, I wanted to say. They pumped his stomach, I was with him the whole time. *Don't tell Father, promise me you won't*, he begged. He wanted to be worthy of you, he didn't want to appear a coward in front of you, he didn't want to turn out to be someone who didn't have the courage to end it all and thus prove himself to his father . . . Well, now I've told you, now I've come out with what I've always kept silent about, his burden, the heavy sack across his shoulders that dragged both of you into an unknown darkness, although it was always clear that you would slip into it—only Pino and I knew that he dare not cross the edge. And when he sensed that I knew that, he convulsively clung to me, without a word, asking me only with his eyes to help him. I've never experienced before such merciless silent pleading; his weight lay also on me, pressing on my neck, gripping me with its tentacles.

Then we took him on that unfortunate holiday to Crete. He wasn't interested in seeing the sights and so we didn't insist, saying let the boy have fun in his own way. He hired a small sailing boat that didn't look particularly safe, but who would have expected the worst? And while you were painting your famous Minotaur in the labyrinth and I was sunning myself and reading Greek art history, we gave him total freedom, we who saw ourselves as such progressive and modern educators. *Will you mend my sail*, he asked, *we're going on a night regatta this evening. It's the first time I've heard of a night regatta*, I said. *I thought it up with the French lot from the next bungalow*, he replied. Then from God knows where that sculptor turned up—what was his name, the one you shared the room with as a student—by coincidence he was also on holiday in Crete with his family. He invited us to his tent, we started drinking, and it was only toward the evening when a strong *Sirocco* blew up that I remembered my promise to Pino and in a befuddled state, drunk on wine and sun, I cynically thought now's the chance for him to prove himself and to cross the line. The *Sirocco* brought with it a real storm; we hid in the sculptor's tent and carried on carousing.

I never told you this, I never dared to speak of the broken promise that drove both of you there, beyond, to the other side. The next morning they came to say that they had found the empty boat; it's funny how a hangover doesn't go away, even when you get some news like that, only worse intoxication, first because of the confusion, then because of the pain. *There's no reason to assume that the torn sail was to blame*, I told myself; *perhaps they'll still find him*, I tried to convince you. They never did find him, although deep inside I feel he's still alive and didn't have the courage to throw himself in for once and for all. You believed to the end that he was swallowed up. Think of Theseus: when he returned home the sailors forgot to raise the white sail and although he was actually still alive, his father Aegeus, thanks to their stupid forgetfulness, threw himself into the sea.

Thanks to my stupid forgetfulness you threw yourself into drink, you dug your own grave because thanks to my stupid forgetfulness you lost a son. And now you ask me how I can go on living? I can, Pino and I were always somehow joint culprits, comrades in the search for a solution for him. I can live because I always have in front of me those hurdles and fences, because I don't grasp at life in the dark unknown as you did, because I don't yearn for death in the dark unknown as Pino did. The hurdles that I haven't cleared I call blind fences, but my unkept promise to Pino I somehow don't count as a blind fence. My next task is your exhibition, Filip; such goals make my life scan like hurdles in a horse race. November next year! Yes, the young custodian filled me with great hope: I'm convinced that he will make a good job of it.

Translated by David Limon

The True Story of Victor Lustig

DANTE WAS RIGHT ON the money when he said there was no greater sorrow than remembering happiness in times of misfortune. If a man is used to starched shirts, good Cuban cigars, suitcases stuffed with money, and drama spiced up with the thrill of new ideas, this gray Alcatraz stench that's eating into my skin becomes an even bigger problem, which I've always had with reality anyway.

That's how it is, mon cher, I said to him, *this pile of iron will finally serve some purpose, and believe me, I know what I'm talking about. I spent practically my entire childhood among the heaps of the scrapyard that my friend's father had back in Czechoslovakia; we would make ourselves guns from rusted bars and wood, there was nothing like it. I hurt myself plenty of times scraping against some protruding rod or trying to put some pieces of metal together to build myself a train. But tell me about yourself, you must've grown up in completely different circumstances,* I prodded.

Well, it was no bed of roses, but I won't complain, he started in a moaning voice, *basically, everything I've earned has been the work of my own two hands, you understand . . . I don't owe anything to anyone and that's not a bad feeling.* Ha, I thought, if he only knew that it's not a bad feeling either when you yourself believe that you're in earnest and that what you've just made up is the gospel truth.

But rule number one is: let the victim get it all off his chest without showing any interest in what he's saying. His last name was Poisson, a real fish, and I was hoping he would take the bait.

59

I told him some story about how the tower was bringing nothing but losses, that it was in need of renovation which would cost more than tearing it down, that it was built for the World's Fair and was never meant to serve any further purpose. *And so I count on your discretion,* I said, taking him by the shoulder in confidence, *talk about the matter as little as possible, the government would like to carry it through as inconspicuously as possible, but there are always going to be some pains in the neck who vehemently complain that it's a waste of public money.* He nodded understandingly. Looking musingly into the distance out of the car window, I saw a man and a woman kissing. Or was the woman pushing the man away? Well, it doesn't matter. *Dear friend,* I said to him, *the Great War is behind us, who knows what else is coming. The army needs artillery, battleships, in short: iron. The industry needs raw material. This is going to be the business of your lifetime, but naturally, everything must remain between us.*

We sat in a black limo, driving along Champ de Mars around the tower rising pompously above the city on its four open legs. *It is ugly,* remarked Poisson, *the government has made the right decision to tear it down, eight thousand tons of spare material, that's no trifling matter.*

Half an hour later, we were already sitting in a café on Rue de la Fédération, drinking cognac. Rule number two that I learned when I was still living in casinos on ocean liners between Europe and America, before the Germans started bombing them: never get wasted, drunkenness can blur your sense of reality. He had no such concerns, he was in for a major deal, prepared to invest big money and put in a handsome sum for my share. He knew that all government people were corrupt, he wasn't that naive, but he didn't have a clue that I was not a government official at all. Five cognacs in, he started sweating and after the sixth, he was perfectly relaxed. Tongue sticky, he said, *When I was a child, my German teacher taught me "table—Tisch, fish—Fisch, porridge—Brei, lustig sein,"* ha, both of us are in that sentence, my last name, meaning fish, and yours, lustig, meaning you're a jolly fellow.

Rule number three: never show you're bored and be a good listener, even if nothing but babble is coming out of your interlocutor's mouth, especially when they get plastered. A studied expression of understanding and attentive listening involves subtly narrowed eyes, a slight occasional nod of the head, arms never crossed. How does it go again? Mundus vult decipi . . . the world wants to be deceived, so let it be conned and swindled. Poisson's blabber subsided, the conversation deflated into silence; I had to stitch it up.

I had a dream about an art collector last night, I began, *one of the pieces he owned was a fifteenth-century painting that he was particularly fond of. It was mounted on a gorgeous carved wooden frame. A wood panel was set in it in place of a canvas, portraying a three-masted bark in a storm. The only problem was that the painting in the frame was so badly damaged by worms that nothing could be done about it. So the owner of the painting found a restorer, who was also something of an artist and forger, and asked him to make another one just like it. Six months later, the painter brought him the copy. They put the original and the imitation on a large table in the collector's drawing room and studied them. Then they took each of them in their hands to examine them from another angle, laid them down again, moved them to the other end of the table, where the light was better, comparing, scrutinizing, trying to spot the slightest difference, but in the end, they had to agree that the paintings were completely identical. Even the fake worm bores were the same. They were thrilled, but not for long. A moment later, they realized they had moved the paintings so many times that they no longer knew which one was the original and which one the replica. Then an idea struck the painter: no harm done, we'll hang them on the wall for a month and the one with a pile of worm dust under it is the original. Said—and done. But a month later, they found a pile of finely chewed wood under both paintings. And so it is,* I said, *we don't know which is the original and which the copy. In the end, all we leave behind is a bit of sawdust.* He burst into a loud guffaw, almost spilling his drink in the process, *what you're saying is the two of us will leave behind a pile of old iron*, he exclaimed, shaking with laughter.

I pretended he was entertaining me, but the truth was I was laughing at the fact that Poisson had taken the bait. You can fulfill all your wishes if you're resourceful enough and dare disturb the universe. Everything that's real is genuine, everything that's real is right; I myself would always see to that, to that poetic side of life. Once, I went to a bank in Missouri and introduced myself as a count, a Habsburg heir, impoverished by the war; they took my word for it and I cashed in the treasury bonds that were nothing but newspaper clippings in a sealed envelope. In order to avoid a scandal, they didn't report me.

Rule number four: never be seen wearing the same shirt twice. Shirts are stamps of trust; each one tells a piece of the story about the person wearing it. The story ends up being what the person wants it to be and what people want to make of it; for no one is forced to form an image of someone by looking at them, people see what they want to see. Kind of like bluffing in poker. They have themselves to blame. Like Mister Capone, who entrusted me with fifty grand to buy illegal booze years ago. I had the money safely deposited in the bank, then returned it to him. *Mister Capone*, I said, *the business went bust.* He was a really honest fellow; because I didn't make off with the dough, he gave me ten percent of the initial sum. Yes, gave it to me. As a gift. Naturally, I made up the whole liquor business.

Hence, André Poisson was a small fish to me. Just two days after our conversation in the café, he brought me a suitcase with money for the iron of the tower that still stands firmly on Champ de Mars, jutting out into the sky above Paris. The following day, I was already sipping champagne in Mariahilferstrasse. Like the Missouri bankers, Poisson was too humiliated to have the guts to sue me. When he found out I had played a trick on him, I explained to him that I was a victim of blackmailing. I still can't believe that he actually felt sorry for me and handed me a leather bag containing a bribe that I was to use to rid myself of my fictitious blackmailer, some corrupt state official.

I returned to Paris. In a few months, I discovered that my idea of comfortable living no longer matched the balance on my bank account. I didn't know what to do and the great tower was still there, immovable, rising over the city, silently and haughtily mocking human incompetence. One day I got tired of being idle and went into action. Pierre, a friend of mine who had a similar taste for pulling tricks, introduced me to a well-to-do fellow with a huffy look, warty skin, and a knack for falling for tricks. Pierre and I organized a random meeting at Café de la Paix, where he brought the Wart Man, *Hey, what are you doing here, come and join us*; after a few amusing platitudes came the pile of old iron, the troublesome tower, *the information is of a confidential nature, you understand, we could be talking handsome profits.* I disliked the Wart Man from the start, but I didn't have much of a choice. First he nodded like a good boy, but when the transfer of documents and the payment were supposed to take place, the police came knocking on the door of the Wart Man's office. They arrested Pierre, telling him, *Your golden days are over, Lustig,* as they cuffed him. I was already running down the fire escape toward the street.

Rule number five: change names and countries. I went to Oklahoma. There I invented a wooden box that prints money. You put in a banknote, wait a few moments, then open the box and pull out another identical banknote. Naturally, I would slip that one in earlier. Unbelievable how some people found that believable. I witnessed astonishment and amazement turning into ecstatic joy. Some sheriff took a particular fancy to the box. He told me that he was involved in an amateur shadow theater, where the actors behind the screen, lighted from behind, held human or animal characters on sticks. He rubbed his hands and paid me a hefty sum for the box. I waved goodbye as his jeep and the magic box inside it bounced away. But in a month, his shadow came looking for me on sleepy mornings in public houses and wild nights in Oklahoma bars, putting me on the other side of its screen, where all my attempts were brought to light, though my name then was Lou Victor Stieg.

And now here I am. In jail on some imaginary island, with nothing but sea around me, the colors on the surface keep changing from one moment to the next, the reflections of the sky on the waves are like illusions hiding fancies. It's bad, so much worse because the stench of misery can't overpower the perfumes of the ladies from Café de la Paix that come back to me when I look toward the coast of San Francisco through the bars of the island prison.

In my case, the contradiction that's supposed to keep life in balance has been a tumble from the comical to the tragic. This annoying feeling that I had wasted my life for anonymous swindling instead of concluding a fictitious contract and becoming a character in a novella, novel, or tragedy and going down in history for all eternity as the man who sold the Eiffel Tower. Twice. But who could write my story the way it really was?

Translated by Špela Bibič

Portugal

I PULL UP IN the parking lot in front of a motel, American-style. Get out and head for the reception desk stashed in a prefabricated cabin of sorts, an extension of the single-story roadside lodging. Behind the motel stretches wasteland, scorched grass, red soil, *tierra tostada por el sol,* from a nearby trashcan wafts a rotting stench.

I push the creaky door aside and walk up to the counter. I arrange my overnight stay in my broken Spanish, the woman hands me the key, and I go to my room.

I throw myself on the bed, exhausted, and go out like a light. I dream of Slovenia, rainy and green, fresh. Of Logarska Dolina, the waterfalls, spruces, mountains, and the azure rivers. I'm flying above them. Then I find myself in Gramma's kitchen, that kitchen where Gramma hunched year after year over her newspaper. And now she's smiling at me, contented, from the crossword puzzle she's solved to the end, as always. Then Gramma is suddenly wearing a white coat with a stethoscope. Startled, I wake up. I look at the ceiling, at the fan hanging from it. This isn't running away, no, it's not running away, it's just something I need to do before I run away for real. Again I fall asleep.

The next day I'm on my way again. I stop at a gas station because the orange light for oil is blinking. That's supposed to be very risky, the engine can stall. A kindly assistant sees to the oil, prods with a stick at the container under the hood and peers at it, soaked in the greasy liquid, as closely as if he were seeing it for the first time, he wipes it clean with a cloth and pumps more gas. I pay, move my car to the side and walk into the station bar. The man behind the counter brings me a cup of coffee, more on the Spanish side, of course, not very strong, and I give him a smile. I can still smile as if nothing were the matter. I can still dissemble. *Dissemble* is a brilliant word, you make yourself resemble someone else and everyone believes that you are what you seem. And you can go on doing it all your life, dissembling, how neat, the verb can be transitive or intransitive. If I've got it right, the bar owner is asking me where I'm going.

Portugal, I answer with another smile, dissembling again.

Ah, Portugal, he repeats, waving it off as if to say, *That's still a ways to go*. A ways, certainly, but I've put the longer part of my way behind me.

Turning on my radio, I listen to the web of dramatic voices reading the news, a tangle of pop songs, and Martian signals. I spend the next night at a motel very much like the first. Maybe the same architect is popular throughout these parts, or maybe they copy each other, it's the same everywhere, the world is nothing but a single village. So who knows why I'm heading precisely for Portugal?

I've had a feeling for that country for . . . I couldn't say, ever since I was little, because it's something different, though I've never been there. Portugal's just a fixation, and that's good enough for me. Now I'm on my way there, at some point I would have had to go anyway and now is certainly the right time, time to do what you have to do, and I for my part have to go to Portugal. Anything else can be done in a hurry, with time slipping away; in fact, the rush helps you clear the tedious chores even if you do it *flightily*, yes, that was Gramma's word. But the things that matter take Time, even if it's five minutes to midnight. Time with a capital T.

I step out of my room when the sun is barely rising. Hah, I, who was always a late sleeper, am now waking up with the birds.

I notice that the car is no longer where I left it the day before. I walk to the reception and have to ring for the receptionist. He waddles in half-asleep and I ask him in English if it was them who moved my car. No, it wasn't them. I pay and walk around the motel corner, true enough, the car is gone, must have been stolen. Once upon a time this would have set my heart pounding in my chest, but now—nothing. Returning to the reception I inquire about the bus, when it's leaving and where from. Close to the motel, just a kilometer away, in an hour. I hoof it to the bus stop, I won't report the theft because I'd give myself away, I told nobody at home that I was going on a journey.

I wait for the first bus. My car has been stolen and once upon a time this would have set my heart pounding in my chest, but now it's disappearing under encroaching malevolent tissue. Yep, once upon a time it would have set my heart pounding.

There is Time. When I saw Gramma last, I didn't know that Time *was*. I left in a rush, as flighty as can be. As if she would go on solving crossword puzzles in the kitchen forever, To imitate, six letters, S-E-M-B-L-E.

When the bus arrives at Aranda de Duero, I ask for the train station because I prefer trains. The station isn't far away, I buy a ticket to Miranda do Douro, the nearest town in Portugal, so as not to pay through the nose for the international connection. I'm going where the Duero river becomes the Douro, where the sunny E shades into a melancholy O. Do the Portuguese yearn in the same way Slovenes do? Our dark green longing, *hrep-enenje*, and their carmine *saudade*. Mournful Portuguese nasals. French nasals are refined and disdainful, Polish are resigned, but Portuguese nasals are sublimely melancholy, just let me hear them and then I can go back.

A man at the deserted train station is eyeing me, curious but not intrusive, looking at my shaved head. Certainly an uncommon sight in a country where hot-blooded women dance the flamenco, passionately tossing their long black curls over their shoulders. I've shaved my head precisely to avoid trouble with hormone-laden guys, I want to be as unattractive as possible, my flirting games are over, irrevocably fled from my interests. Over. No longer wearing tribal jewelry, I look more like a Buddhist monk with an army backpack and baggy pants, consider me a sexless creature, a neuter gender journeying to the end of the day.

Like a man pressing after a woman, the Intercity train is eagerly following the merry Duero, which is about to flow and transform into a different current, dissembling as a mournful Douro. I've taken up smoking again. I quit ten years ago, but now, at thirty, I light a *ducado* with as much passion as in those black-and-white movies. The Duero is greenish-brown but in Portugal it may be black, as black as the end of the day.

In the corridor of the squalid train I'm dragging on my second *ducado* when a young man steps from the next-door compartment. He seems pleasant. When he speaks to me, I let him know that I don't understand much Spanish. We communicate partly in English, partly in his language. *¿Donde?*—Portugal.—*Ah, Portugal. ¿Porqué?* The overwhelming question. I might as well tell him, he will never see me again, I needn't be embarrassed. No, he will never see me again, at least not in my lifetime.

At the border enters a customs officer, carelessly glancing through the papers. When he comes to me, he stops and reaches for my Slovene passport, he's never seen one before, he studies it both inside and outside and smiles. I smile too, dissembling.

The train runs into the land of Portugal. Here I am, almost at the end of the day, the dark is falling and nobody knows where I am, except maybe Gramma.

I get off at Miranda do Douro and buy a new ticket. I have to disembark, just as I have to dissemble. A dis-embarker and dis-sembler, I don't know how I shall dissemble next. The Douro is not black, or is this a mere mirage? Perhaps it is black but still perceived as brownish-green by my human eyes. Or greenish-brown, is there a difference?

Yes, straight to Lisbon, Porto can wait, it's second in line. That, at least, is the advice I've gleaned from Tabucchi's *Requiem*. But now, now it seems to me that it's not possible to misunderstand . . . that it's all right to understand in our own way. Once I was bursting with doubts and uncertainties, now the uncertainty is only one, enormous.

Vineyards, cork oaks, red soil, bland white villages with shutters closed. That's why I've come, the closed shutters, I've come to peer through the cracks of Southern Europe's most reclusive people, to prise open the shutters of the almost-MediTerranean, Mid-Earth, where we were born. The shutters closing on a mystery. Gramma knows it already and I'll know it soon, that great uncertainty shuttered off from a beating sun. And when the day sets, the shutters are flung open for a breath of fresh night.

Coimbra. Two women in the corridor are chatting in an unfathomable language, then one gets off and the remaining woman is evidently bored. Her hair gathered into a bun, she is glancing around for someone to talk to. Catching sight of me, she waves her handkerchief as if to signal how hot it is on the train. I nod and she says something. I shrug my shoulders as if to say that I don't understand. *A foreigner?—Yes, a foreigner.—Lisbon?—Yes, Lisbon.* Not so reclusive really, they're small and dark, the Portuguese, like imps.

He told me gravely, *Well, we've run all the tests now, the results from the Oncology Institute have come as well.* It's better to be before and better to be after, but that very moment is terrible, just so that you'll know if it happens to you. That moment is the worst, then it dissolves. After a while everything clears up and you know exactly the things you still have to do. Without rush, and certainly without flightiness.

We arrive in Lisbon. Finding a nearby restaurant, I order tripe and a glass of honey wine. I was always partial to red, but now I decline the Porto as too sugary for what I'm going through. From the restaurant terrace, from the Lisbon citadel, I'm looking at the sea. What more could one ask for?

I want to get aboard a tram, no matter what. I sit down on a wooden bench, a gentleman with a threadbare briefcase under his arm reminds me of Tabucchi's Mr. Pereira. Pereira had never thought of death before.

Above Portugal, in Galicia, lies a cape called Finisterre. End of the earth, end of the world. Unique as it may sound, there's a Finistère in France too, now, which is the right one?

I'm walking in the Lisbon streets, not in the least afraid of drug dealers. Now that I look like a narkie myself, shaved head and all, now that I'm sauntering at leisure through the streets rising toward the sun, they're even offering me their stuff. Once upon a time it would have set my heart pounding but now nothing happens, they can do nothing to me, fate has drafted a different plan. Like the night when I told him I was sick and I saw that he couldn't stick with me, and then wandered alone in the dark all over town, when I was afraid of no potential criminal because the wound was too deep for anyone to dare attack me. They would have seen at once that I was no suitable victim, I, who had always dreaded walking alone at night more than anything.

Metastases are visible on the right cerebral hemisphere and on the left lung epithelium, said the white man. Once upon a time this set my heart pounding, but not any longer. The doctor closed his folder, my file, as if to say, *The case is closed.*

The air is mellow, dry, salty, the people are relaxed but not loud, everything is so natural. This is why I've come. The sun is tinged with honey, like wine, and lottery tickets are being sold in the Largo da Estrela.

Yes, the case is closed. I'm in Lisbon. This is my *finis terrae.* The tripe in sauce was excellent, perhaps a little heavy on the stomach but excellent. In the café, a meeting place of the locals, yellow wine flows smoothly down my throat into the left lung atrium. The sea in the distance is dark brown, almost black. Barges are sailing out, out into the open, saying farewell with mournful, nasal honks. Darkness is falling. All I need to do now is find a place for the night.

A House of Paper

Ride la stella Aldebaran, ride e fa:
to be, to be, to be or not to be
ride la stella, ride e fa: trallallà
to be, to be, to be or not to be

Paolo Conte, *l'Orchestrina (Nelson)*

IT WAS BACK LAST summer that I noticed I was shrinking. First
by my clothes, by my long sleeves and pant legs, by my skirt
falling below the knee rather than just above it, then by my
shoes, in which my toes could suddenly not just wiggle up and
down but Charleston left and right. This summer, my feet are
swimming in their sandals, tripping me up as I walk down the
summer pavement, with the greasy white lines of pedestrian
crossings turning to bright dashes, exclamation marks, hyphens,
the clouds stretching out at times into revision marks, unspaced,
bold, italic, change the word order and the weather will change.
All this meddling of alien hands and eyes with texts is changing
the atmosphere, delaying the regular comet arrivals, undermin-
ing the psyche of translators, let alone authors.

As a translator, I bear my share of the guilt as well. With my
own perspective and idio-whatever, I interfere ("grossly interfere"
is the most common phrase) with authorial creations, counter-
feiting them in another language. Perhaps this shrinking is my
punishment for defacing all the books I've translated—over the
last fifteen years mainly the works of a single author, the famous
Janus Carta. I'm the one to sift each of his words, turn it around,
inspect it from all sides, sniff at it, even correct it with a faint

twinge of conscience, that is, find a better equivalent when the rush of the narrative dulls the author's sensitivity to detail. But we, dissecting them to the bone, we drudges know every one of their weaknesses, we know where the blind fool has repeated a word for the third time on the page, we contract "she is cooking, and when dinner is ready" into "when she has cooked dinner," smiling maternally in our bitter solitude at each improvement. All writers should be proficient in another language and translate themselves into it—then they would see how thankful they should be for our hair-splitting *acribia*. After all, they can't expect us to shoulder the blame for their own shortcomings!

And now, having noted for some time that I'm shrinking, I wonder if it might be a visitation of St. Jerome for my translator's sins. At first I blamed it on the sun and took to keeping in the shade, then I settled on clothes that were a size smaller, and on shoes that were too. I didn't panic until I dreamed one night that I had shrunk almost to the point of disappearance. Frightened, I sent Janus Carta a postcard: *Dear Janus, I've just translated your* House of Paper *and am now enjoying my holiday. The publisher assures me that it will come out by the end of September. Best wishes . . .* I was one of the few who knew his real address, everyone else had to contact him by fax. It was his clever way of evading the pests who badgered him daily with three-hundred-page novels, asking for recommendations.

I had only met Janus a couple of times. His sharp nose sniffed out at once that I was single. A woman who could devote much of her time—all of it, in fact—to transplanting his oeuvre to another language. A woman with no other self-affirmation in her life. A woman perhaps secretly in love with her translatee. Paper eroticism, Platonic pedestals, repressed elective affinity. A woman with a life unlived, with just the devotion needed to transfer his greatness intact to readers in her own language.

It was Janus who suggested a blood test in his letter, after I had complained about my perceived shrinkage and my fear of it. *It doesn't flow through our veins for nothing*, he wrote in his slanting hand, which pressed on toward a pathetically yearning future, *it carries secret messages under the parchment-like epidermis*. Strange that he didn't use the more poetic verb *course*. Anyway, I mustered up courage and went to the health center, holding the author's imaginary hand in mine. Watching blood drops oozing into the test tube like wine lees, I agonized over what those young lab assistants would learn about me: decoding from the blood molecules and chemistry formulas who I was, what I wanted, and where I was headed, they would give me sage looks and most likely never tell me the truth. I would leave feeling stupid, with no more knowledge about myself, while they would look after me, joining their heads together and shaking them in disapproval. But in fact the doctor admitted that he was puzzled by my reduction, *reductio corporis* was how he put it technically, the first perhaps to have introduced this medical term. He told me to have my height measured at his office every month, and promised to pay particular attention to my case—to give lectures on it to his students, perhaps even at an all-important symposium in Tokyo, to which he aspired to be invited in five years. What I hope is that I'm not reduced to a Thumbelina by then, accompanying him to Japan in a glasses or cell phone case, like a showcase Lilliputian.

What I feared was losing not only my size but my memory as well: losing my memories, knowledge, skills. What if the reduced size of my brain robbed me of my full self-awareness, what if my linguistic knowledge cocooned in an imperceptible pore within some microscopic curve of my brain, never to be teased out again? A midget, I would squeak out sentences that could never hold or know a subordinate clause, let alone speculate on the simplest structural feature of another language. Janus Carta, partly concerned that the numbing fear might hinder my intensive translating, and partly, no doubt, fed up with me, tried to dismiss all my worries with: *My dear lady, if you're to remain tall, you must hold up your head*. It was easy for him to talk: I was the smaller one in any case.

Even after his death. Yes, soon afterward rumors spread that
he was ill. Worried as I was, I didn't dare ask him outright,
hoping that he would reveal more in his letters, in his replies
to my questions about what the hell he had meant with a word
that could have several meanings in our language. And before I
had gathered the nerve to inquire after his health directly, news
came from his country of the unexpected demise of a great artist, matchless aesthete, and candidate for, or winner of, several
prestigious international literary prizes.

On hearing the news I seemed to shrink even more. My
summer straw hat began dancing around the circle of my head,
its brim slipping over my eyes. Where is the disappearing part
of me going? Perhaps I'm evaporating in the white sun, the
growing vacuum around me licking at my own edges, as fire
licks at paper. I had always believed that I was doing something
meaningful, something great in its smallness, that I was a Vestal
Virgin of literary truth, a dictionary priestess in the service of
Our Lords the Authors, a pious servant shuffling the carefully
considered words that were engraved in books for all eternity. I
had always wondered what it was like on the other side, in the
world of a fool's freedom, where you can build yourself a house
of paper written all over and simply live in it, and if you've built
well, others come respectfully knocking on the door of your
paper home, curiously peeping in to see if the writing inside is
the same as outside. I had always wondered how it feels to be an
author, how it feels when, halfway between your idea and your
recording hand, a great fraud happens at the world's expense. Do
you sleep peacefully, counterfeiter? Are you haunted by illusions,
fictions, dreams? Are you real to yourself, or are you fading away
into the white page, from whose milky light you can always
emerge to reveal yourself in hazy outlines?

After Janus Carta's death this summer, there was no book-
shop window that didn't display his books. In my translation,
naturally. He was discussed in cultural features on the radio and
TV, in newspapers and their literary supplements. He sold like

hot cakes, to be served with all kinds of tea. Disseminated in death, his sentences were blown like dandelion clocks to the City and the World: now he was heard of where he had previously been unknown. I, for my part, went on shrinking. The advantage was that it gave me a good excuse for a brand-new summer wardrobe, especially a swimsuit. I followed the hot summer's cultural news on holiday at the seaside, my first real holiday because there was no more steady work for me to do; I had translated everything of Carta's there was to translate, so I could take a break now. And I was no longer pestered by anyone wanting to contact him. No one was interested in his fax number anymore.

I was sitting under a night sky in front of the pension, talking to people I had met at the seaside: to a historian uncovering the massacres after World War II and his wife discovering the pangs of post-forty aging, to a chatty cyclist who rode his bike to the beach every day, and to an elderly couple—to him, with his hair dyed a new color this year, and her, who had replaced the gentleman's escort from the year before. They were flattered to know the translator of a famous author they hadn't heard of until two months ago. We were sitting under the dark olive trees facing the sea, and the talkative cyclist said, *It looks like Taurus has shrunk: if we could see his eye in the summer, the star Aldebaran, it would certainly crumple up on itself, though it would go on giving an intense light.* He was the most perceptive of the bunch, the cyclist, the others were just nodding, bluffing their way through. Every now and then he would glance at my diminished breasts.

The evening and night were lit up by fireflies, whose cool, constant light is produced by a chemical reaction. As with glowworms: I saw a documentary on them once, worms hanging like stars from the ceilings of black subterranean caves, lowering deadly sticky threads to trap spiders and other unfortunates wandering into this Hades. That evening and night were the most peaceful in my life.

Autumn in the city, just as dazzling as the summer, was more eventful. Soon after arriving home, I had a phone call from a Mr. Henk, who introduced himself as Carta's lawyer. He claimed to have found some things, some notes to do with me. I was annoyed by the prospect of more hassle with Carta, who wouldn't let me rest even when he was gone. Still, I journeyed to the neighboring country to see Mr. Henk, who peered at me sagely from behind his mahogany desk. *This portfolio is for you,* he said, *papers and such, and also this key—before he died, you see, he told me to give you the key to his summer cottage, which is hardly bigger than this room, to straighten things out. By Carta's orders, I used to send a boy from a technical firm there to feed paper through the window—all he had to do was open the shutters and undo the lock on the window frame—into the house, or rather into a device inside, endless paper, but don't take it literally, it's just a phrase, paper can never be endless.*

Paper could never be endless? H'm. And I should go there to straighten things out? That was a good one. How could Carta expect anything more from me now that he was dead, even if it was death that had made him eternal and endless like his paper? How could he expect more than the faithfulness I had already bestowed on him?

The day was brilliant, the summer was Indian, and the cottage of Janus Carta on the hill was white—how much lovelier it must have looked in the black northern gale. I trudged uphill, my feet blistered from my new shoes, again a size smaller, and from the distance the house seemed encrusted, as if held upright by cardboard, or salt, or invisible threads running up to Aldebaran, the invisible star from the cyclist's conversation. Winded, I reached the door, fished out the key and tried to unlock it, but it seemed to be stuck or else forced into place by an unknown power, the natural force of air or water or vacuum. I went on pushing with all my might, and suddenly a multilayered lava of paper sheets slid out from behind the door. I tossed them aside, not minding at the time that they could be blown away, so eager was I to see what lay inside. Trying to clear a passage for the door, I removed a fair amount of paper. Machine-typed pages. Tired, I sat down in front of the house and picked up a few. All of them were headed by a date, a strange code, and the sender's name.

All had been faxed.

The fax. Carta's fax. His one means of receiving unwanted mail from the pests. Requests for an interview, for a feature in some magazine or other, for a recommendation; letters from budding writers eager for publication; texts by potential talents, by never-to-be literary stars. Anything that would have distracted Janus from his creative work had been channeled into this cottage where he had shut away the outside world. And as the lawyer had said, someone had regularly come to feed paper into the fax machine. Endless paper.

There was no stopping me in my zeal. It was morning and I had the whole day left to burrow my way to the answer.

In the red glow of evening, having emptied enough of the cottage to make sure that it contained nothing else but a little table for the fax machine and two old thesauri, I sat down, sweating, on a patch of grass still bare of paper, and opened a can of beer. The wind danced among the pages, playfully mixing them in an insoluble rebus. I smiled and raised the can in a toast toward the sky, *You are there, Janus, aren't you?*

The answer arrived like a paper airplane, folded in class by a schoolboy and sent flying into the teacher's face. I'm being eroded by the outside world through the epidermis, the magic circle of my skin, and you, you packed that world into a cottage to grow rampant in its interior, to fill its guts like a tumor while leaving you untouched. You were alone in yourself to the last, while I'm dwindling to nothing, running out, running out of words to describe it all.

I phoned Carta's lawyer, asking him to order a truck to take away all that cellulose, written all over with the desires and pleas and dreams of people I would never meet. Take the whole pile to the dump, or else shake it from the truckbed into the backyard of some zealous Carta biographer. But Mr. Henk would have none of it: for him, he said, *In re Carta* was closed. I switched off my phone, alone in the waning light with the layers of letters and words and sentences struggling for expression on the white paper, the only bright spot left in the twilight. I struck a match, bent down, and felt the mellow warmth of the pages slowly being consumed. The fire roamed across them as if to read every single one and take it along into the sooty sky, reddened by the transient light of the flames. Surely there would be a final full stop to this oeuvre, too.

Ramón de Caballo

WHEN I RETURNED TO Santiago de las Vegas more than forty years later, the pale dream images which I'd been carrying in myself cleared both before and within my eyes, cruelly and mercilessly. I visited the Biblioteca pública y Archivo and rummaged for papers bearing witness to the fact that my parents had once lived there, a couple of scientists of whom the place may well be proud even today, but I found precious little, nothing but a handful of local chronicle notices and newspaper references of forty years ago. *Books have been disappearing, someone's been stealing them, very cleverly, we can't catch them at it*, said the gray-gowned librarian, *They probably sell them someplace else*, he said and rubbed his forehead, concerned. At a loss for a reply, I shook his hand and took my leave.

I sought out the old patio surrounding the lush, column-lined garden, it was there that Mother used to grow her plants and inspect them every morning, lifting the magnifying lens to her face and endowing her eye with horrifying proportions.

I visited my father's lab where he used to dissect his field crops long years ago, it was opened for me by a neighbor who knew who I was, he was frail and gnarled and I hadn't forgotten him either, even if very young children are supposed to remember nothing. To me, though, everything seemed as fresh as yesterday, and I'm sure it wasn't just because of what I'd later heard about the place: it was because of the images which I'd carried in myself all that time and finally came back to return—back to my island native town, miles and miles away from my present home.

The pots in which Father used to propagate vanilla were still there, although they no longer stood on tables in a greenhouse but were neatly stacked by the wall, Father used to study them with so much love, a love he'd never have bestowed on my mother, and Mother peered through her microscope with a passion she had never granted to my father. It was in such a family that I grew up, the son of an agronomist and a botanist, the son of bio-yearners.

But I, too, passionately loved a plant, one single plant, I loved not one single plant species but one single tree, a *Trophis racemosa* in the middle of our patio—I hadn't been able to climb it before because I'd been too little—a "horse branch," *ramón de caballo*. My parents talked to me about it with the eros that was missing between them, with true Cuban nostalgia and with their own, unique, treesickness. Fortunately I hadn't inherited their professional and almost painful hankering after vegetation, but, needless to say, I'd been thoroughly imbued by it, that treesickness, so much so that in my teenage years I adopted a poor substitute, an oak which grew in front of the house at the other end of the world, the house where we returned after several years on the paradise isle.

My passion was not the consuming chlorophyll ardor of my parents. My *passione* was imagination seasoned with science fiction, with bygone worlds and with a constellation of rational figments. To the latter certainly belongs my father's and mother's photosynthesis heritage, which curbs my wantonness, my *No, Don't want to, I said I don't want to and that's the bottom line*— my *No* on the afternoon when I was ten and refused a plate of escargots set on the table by Conchita, a maid who'd come with us from faraway exotic places: no, I don't want the bloody snails forced on me by father and mother, a couple of nature freaks.

I ran out of the dining room straight into the garden and clambered up the fatherly oak, which received me in its motherly branches, I'll stay here, I'll stay here till the end of time.

Staunchly, with the unwearying stubbornness of an adolescent who has been uprooted from paradise at a tender age and transplanted into a warm but often unkind climate, with the defiance of one who is rebelling because rebellion is ultimately his only *raison d'être*, with the resistance of a fighter for the universe, I declared that I wasn't going to eat slimy slugs and climbed a tree where I could talk to the brothers of those snails, or so I imagined at least, I knew that I was infinitely right and that my parents were abysmally wrong; this firm conviction was interwoven with a feeling of guilt, with uncertainty, with pride and a what-if-it's-not-quite-like-that, what-if-there's-more-to-it-than-meets-the-eye doubt.

This scene trickled in before my eyes when, forty years later, I was again watching the *ramón de caballo*, a mulberry tree much lordlier than my oak, a tree which had belonged to me, had been destined for me, but which I'd had to abandon at three, a tree on top of which I'd certainly have driven home my belief much more effectively, for it would have taken me under its wings, saying, That's the way to think and none other, the way you're thinking, and That's the way to stand up, exactly the way you've chosen, *bravo, ¡valor!, ¡ánimo!*, atta boy, show'em what you've got.

At first it seemed only a game that would last an hour, two perhaps. But when I was spending my second day on the oak, my mother came to plead with me, distraught, from underneath the lowest branch to return to the house and eat with them. What happened afterward is more or less adroitly, more or less imaginatively, described in a book I published when I was more than grown-up and mature and—sadly—no longer prone to such silly tricks, but fortunately they were preserved in my heart, whereas the scientific temperament which I was expected to inherit was not.

In short, I was planted in Cuba and uprooted and transplanted to San Remo at three. San Remo, Italy. For you it probably conjures up pop songs, but for me it's *nina nana nina o* and *ambarabà ciccì coccò*, rhymes with which our Conchita, planted by my parents, like myself, in a different part of the world, used to sing me to sleep. Europe! Europe! That meat-slicer, that straw-shredder of ideas, so different from and yet so oddly like the ideas emerging from the warm soil of Latin America, burgeoning and curling into flounces and garlands; that processor of uncurbed ideas, primal and carnal in sultry places but elsewhere stalked by the Hyperboreans, who are transforming them into crystal cubes and trying to blow into them some suppressed life. And yet, on the other hand: Europe! Europe! Her coldness squeezes the best out of you, you reduce yourself to reason and warm yourself up with rum in a boat cabin stuffed with the cigarette smoke of inveterate bohemians, friends of the gray sea on which you're sailing, driven by the power of sentiment. That's my take on that old lady of a continent, both bad and good, I'm a Cuban and a European, but, above all, in both cases a Latino. As a newborn baby I was laid into one of Europe's oldest cradles, Italy, an old lady but today nonetheless the youngest among the continental countries, crisscrossed by the patter of childish people, its soil at times trodden on by some sage respected by all and heard by none.

In fact I wanted to describe one more event from the time I returned to Santiago de las Vegas after forty years and took walks to our former Colonial-style house, which had surprisingly remained empty all that time. One morning I glimpsed there a girl, she sneaked to my undestined tree, drew from her poncho-like mantle a small jar, and scattered under my *ramón de caballo* a kind of dust. The incident wouldn't have stuck in my memory if I hadn't caught her once again, two days later, so the third time I armed myself with the cracked pocket binoculars that I'd found in a chest in my old home and always brought along whenever I came to visit. It took a week before the stranger showed up again, and through the steamy lens I could see that the vessel from which she was pouring resembled an urn, and the gray dust ashes.

How many dead does she bury per week to have so much material? I joked when I was telling of my unusual experience to my parents' friends, the Ochoa family, where I was a regular dinner guest in those days. *Could be a serial killer*, guffawed the father, Rodrigo, *Maybe she's got a blocked fireplace*, suggested Maria Eva, *Maybe . . .* began old Pilar but then just waved it off.

I couldn't sleep that night, whether it was the girl with the urn, the full moon, or simply that I didn't have much to do in Santiago de las Vegas and my homesickness, real or imagined, was compounded by boredom in a couple of weeks. I was tossing and turning, mulling over the Cuban girl's bizarre behavior. And as I had little better to do than stroll around Santiago, dine with the Ochoas, rummage through the local library and archives, or haunt the El Conde cafe, I decided to unravel the terrible mystery. Terrible . . . as I'd trumped it up in my idleness.

For several days running I lay in ambush, in vain. On Saturday evening I joined the party in front of the town hall, hoping to see her there, once more in vain. I tore myself from the dancing crowd of townspeople and headed for our dark house. I sat down on the deserted steps leading to the entrance door and lit a cigarette, the match crackled in the silence which was backed only by the faraway sound of the local orchestra, the light coming from the direction of the accordion tones. I waited.

I waited. There was a rustle, she knelt down under my tree and, drawing the oval jar from a bundle, opened the lid and began to strew the powdery contents all over the tree roots.

I rose and made my way toward her, she heard me and looked around in alarm, but before she even thought of flight I stood before her and struck another match to light her up, she was not pretty, was my first impression, her thick glasses spoiled her looks, she gave me an awkward smile and greeted me in embarrassment with *¡buenas noches!*. *What are you doing, fertilizing the ramón de caballo*, I asked, *Ramón de caballo*, she repeated, surprised, her eyes wide open behind the thick lenses, and just then her metal container dropped to the ground. Seizing the opportunity, I swooped to pick it up. *What's this, it looks like a canister or my mom's last abode*, I asked, pointing at the object, but she snatched it from my hand, evidently irritated by my gallows humor. *Who are you*, she asked, *I'll tell you if you tell me what you're doing here*, I dickered. Wordless, she walked over to the steps leading to the entrance gate and sat down. *My name is Juanita.*

I sat down next to her. *Pleased to meet you, my name is C., I. C.*, I said, inadvertently echoing the great spy, my name is the name of my country. *I used to live here more than forty years ago, we moved out when I was just three. This is my former home*, I said, pointing at the house behind us, *I don't know where I'm at home or to which country I belong, the first or the second, I'm a plant without roots, a book with two beginnings.* I didn't want to tire her with Europes and Americas. *H'm*, she smirked and glanced at her urn. I looked at her inquiringly. *Do you have anything to do with books*, she challenged me. *I'm a writer, believe it or not*, I answered ironically and she smiled back, with a cynical expression on her face. We both knew that the style of the game was set.

What do you write, she asked, looking at me askance. *All sorts of fibs and figments*, I countered. *Sounds familiar*, she retorted. *And you, what are you doing with this little pot at this time of night under my tree?*

Under your tree?

Under my tree. Under the tree of rebellion and growing up, under my tree which had helped me straighten the distorted lens for looking at the world, under the tree of pallid dream images. *Once upon a time there lived a boy who wouldn't eat escargots for lunch, so he climbed on an oak tree in the garden and refused to come down, everyone was pleading with him but he remained on the tree and . . .*

And?

The thick glass lenses flashed curiosity, *I'm a poor speaker, you'd better read it for yourself, the title of the book is . . .* Her expectations peaked and I knew that I'd gained the upper hand. *I'll tell you if you explain to me what you were doing here?*

She bit her lip. *I was scattering ashes under your ramón de caballo.*

You don't say, I answered with obviously faked surprise. A dark confidentiality was growing between us, a gloomy sympathy. *I'm very angry,* she continued, *so angry that I've turned into a proper pyromaniac. I like to burn. Burn books.*

Cristo della Madonna! Certainly, some author of Latin American figments would know how to weave this into a story. I was flabbergasted but concealed it well. Through my mind flashed Alexandria, the *Kristallnacht* and *Fahrenheit 451.* I knew she was telling the truth. *Books? What books?*

All the books that rile me up. Aren't you ever outraged by a book? I was left speechless.

It started with the university reading list, there's nothing more maddening than endnotes. The stove at home suited my purpose to a T, but it had to be cleaned up later or Father might have smelled a rat, you've no idea how much ash can pile up! Then I found your tree, really convenient, the house hasn't been lived in for years . . . and there must be a ritual too, with an urn, you have to be respectful, a book is still a book and you can't just scatter it into the wind.

It continued with bad translations, there are quite a few of those, too, with too-small print, incomplete encyclopedias . . . back then they were still on loan at the Biblioteca pública y Archivo, but later they must have suspected something.

What about ugly front covers, I nearly enthused. *Oh, those too,* she confirmed with relief, *though in those cases I usually just burned the covers. But I don't burn books for ideological reasons, it's a symbolic act, although . . . the best bonfire of all was* What

Every Newlywed Wife Should Know *from the thirties. The poetry collections of certain parvenus and upstarts I won't even mention. Or boring biographies . . .*

I was beginning to be almost amused. *You wouldn't believe it, the ashes of a Bildungsroman look like snow in the Andes,* she warmed to her story, *and the burned collected works of a local writer that I won't name looked like oatflakes.*

Are you playing at censorship, I grew serious, *why won't you let such books exist as well?*

A matter of taste, she stated with confidence, *I'm not dangerous, I never burn more than one copy of each work; have you got another cigarette?* I tapped my fingers against the pack, making a cigarette pop out. As I slid a match against the brown side of the box, the flame doubled in her thick glasses. My mother had worn such glasses, too, the glasses of a rational scientist, and next to me in the warm night was now sitting a girl whose rationality was twisting into untrammeled peculiarity. In a creepy way I liked her, the girl, even if I was frightened by her doings: at last I felt that my visit and the long days spent in Santiago de las Vegas had not been useless, that I had actually lived to see something new. I wasn't going to preach at her, her gaze would have set me on fire like a *Bildungsroman*, my ashes would have bleached the branches of my tree, like hoarfrost whitening the Cordilleras.

We said farewell when dawn was already breaking and the music on the dance floor before the town hall had died out. The day heated up to a glow and the sun began to scorch people, animals, and houses, we burned in its fire but didn't burn up.

Drenched in sweat, I boarded a plane the next day, and as we hovered above the clouds, quite close to the orangey ball, I thought of my tree. It was not just my imaginary tree of rebellion: for Juanita it was the burying ground for everything offensive, under it she fulfilled her wanton dreams, fertilizing it with her resistance, her child's irresponsibility. That was what I mused upon, returning to the morphology of my old landscapes.

Roma Termini

TRA-TAM, TRA-TAM, THE TRAIN wheels are rattling in the rhythm of a song which Vuka starts singing under her breath, *mene je majka dojila, džanum*, I was nursed by my mother, O my soul, *mene je majka, džanum, doji-i-i-la*, a song that surfaces in Vuka's mind on the Intercity train from Trieste to Rome. The landscape is rushing past her as if to elude her, and her neighbor's nodding head is drooping toward her left shoulder as if trying to slip away from its owner. Tra-tam, tra-tam, rattles the train, steadily pressing on through the landscape and following the tracks, just as she used to run as a little girl along the white lines painted on the stadium racetrack. Now Papa is lying there, resting in her stadium, the graveyards were so full that people were being buried in the outdoor gym instead.

A black-dressed, angular lady with a red shawl enters the compartment, asking if the seat by the door is free. Good thing I know Italian, thinks Vuka to herself, or I'd be even more lost. *Did you see Rome?* a neighbor asked her brother Vojo on the tip of the Pelješac peninsula, after lifting him high by the ears. *No*, answered Vojo incredulously, and the neighbor repeated the operation. *Did you see it now?* he asked, lowering him again. Vojo shook his head, and the neighbor lifted him for the third time. *And now, did you see the eternal city?* he wanted to know, and Vojo hastily confirmed. All of a sudden Italy no longer seems as fabulous as it did on that Pelješac holiday, when they tried to glimpse it across the sea's surface. She had strained her eyes so long that she finally did seem to make out, just above the sea, the mountain skyline of a faraway land where princes and princesses walked and winged white horses flew.

She has relatives waiting for her in Rome, she'll stay with them until it crystallizes what's to be done with her. *Good thing I've studied Italian though I haven't graduated because of the war,* she thinks again, thanks to her Italian she'd been able to earn a living by interpreting for Italian journalists, she'd simply walked into the crumbling building of the Holiday Inn and asked at the reception desk if anyone needed a translator, and the receptionist referred her to the team of the RAI, the national Italian television. First the cameraman thrust a map and pencil in her hands, telling her to mark the dangerous districts, and Vuka warily colored Ilijaš, Vogošča, Grbavica, Hadžiše, Ilidža, Dobrinja, and Pale. Then they drove her around and she had to translate every word, even when someone just sighed, even worse, sometimes they didn't listen to her at all, they had the nerve to misread the sign *Pazi, snajper, Watch out, sniper,* during a direct broadcast, and the head journalist dramatically reported that the besieged city had been reduced to naming its squares after snipers, *Piazza Sniper.* Vuka didn't know whether to laugh or cry, she raised her hands but dropped them again in resignation, why drag her along at all if they knew everything best?

With a drawn-out screech the Intercity stops at Florence, Vuka peers through the window and spots a stray dog roaming the platform. He looks like Vojo's sheepdog who disappeared during the war. Your Mama had him put down because you couldn't feed him any longer, a neighbor woman told her, but Vuka couldn't believe a thing so cruel of her mother, so she and Vojo searched for Aron all over town in the growing hordes of stray animals. The dog is gone, so is Papa, thank goodness she still has Mama and Vojo or she'd be even more frightened than she is, and frightened she has always been, even before the war, she was born with it, the fear. The train pulls out again, tra-tam, tra-tam, the wheels are rattling in the rhythm of the

song which Vuka is singing under her breath, *zatoj sam tanka,
visoka, džanum*, that's why I'm slender, tall, O my soul, *zatoj sam
tanka, džanum, vis-o-o-o-ka*. Her fellow passenger's head painfully bumps against her gaunt shoulder, the man's eyelids, glued
together, blink and he shifts his weight to the other side. The
greenery is thickening into streaks brushing against the train,
the trees and bushes are flashing past Vuka's window, sprinting
as Vuka used to sprint along the left bank of the Miljacka River
till her mother sold the snow-white sneakers which had been
her pride. The only jogger she continued to see by the river was
that nutty, bald old man, every day at the same hour, in ceasefire
and under fire, he wouldn't allow himself to be disturbed, to
be stripped of his iron habit, this was his resistance against the
occupying force, a surviving scrap of civilization in a maddened
world, a normality which defied the extreme circumstances.

Tra-tam, tra-tam, the train wheels are rattling in the rhythm
of the song Vuka starts singing under her breath. *Tickets, please*,
says the conductor, and all passengers in the compartment start
rummaging in their bags and pockets, Vuka's neighbor wakes up
and glances around, bleary-eyed, *he's as cool as a cucumber*, Vuka
thinks, *definitely not as scared as me, he doesn't know the primal
fear coursing through one's marrow*. The elderly black-dressed lady
with the red shawl, sitting by the door, gives Vuka a curious
once-over as if she recognized her for a foreigner, as if she saw
through her and eyed the innate fear in her bones. *She knows
what it's all about*, Vuka reflects, leaning against the headrest to
suppress the chill creeping over the back of her head.

The train arrives at an enormous railway station. Vuka waits
for everyone to get off, then clambers from the train herself.
Small and helpless she drags her suitcase behind, trudging under
the huge sign ROMA TERMINI. Coming behind is the easy-
going gentleman from her compartment, in front she notices the
black-dressed lady with the red shawl set her two suitcases on the
ground and snap her fingers for two shady-looking individuals

who run up to her, skinny and pockmarked and glassy-eyed, Vuka believes this must be how junkies look. In the crowd she loses sight of both fellow passengers and when she walks from the railway station, she is enveloped in the city hubbub. Vuka sits down on her suitcase, waiting, waiting to be picked up by her relatives as agreed.

More than an hour later, Vuka is treading alone by the Roman houses, the homey clatter of plates ringing through the open windows, it's lunchtime but this sound is more alien now than anything else in the world. *This is exile*, she thinks, anxiety constricts her breast and she strives desperately to recall her room, her nursery that had been crammed with toys but a few years ago, but she can't. *Wherever you go, always carry it with you*, said Uncle Nešo, giving her a little silver dolphin on a chain, Uncle Nešo, who had marched from Srebrenica with a single white plastic bag. *And he, what sort of amulet was he wearing to protect him from all harm*, wonders Vuka, looking for a bench to sit down, and bitterly recalls that she had left the dolphin at home.

I'd better go back to the station, she thinks—in fact she doesn't even know where her Roman relatives' street is—and trudges back, exhausted. Pulling a carefully folded piece of paper with the address from her pocket, she asks a *carabiniere* about the bus. On his advice she takes the escalator into the bowels of the train station where the subway runs, and queues up to buy a ticket. She is standing at the end of a slowly dwindling tail, when she suddenly notices two weird-looking guys on each side of the ticket booth, heavily pockmarked and glassy-eyed. She remembers that they helped carry the luggage of her spindly, black-dressed fellow passenger with the red shawl, after she'd summoned them with a snap of her fingers. The guys, both in front of the booth now, give her the once-over, then exchange looks. *Mene je majka dojila, džanum*, I was nursed by my mother, O my soul, Vuka tries to sing under her breath for courage, but her voice feebly wriggles from her breast, twisting in her mouth. The people in the queue are scattering fast like threaded beads, Vuka stalks up to the ticket booth to conceal the fearful wobbling of her legs, but she is suddenly enveloped by fear, a fear blowing through her, imbuing her, Vuka runs away, *zatoj sam tanka, rumena, džanum*, that's why I'm slender, rosy, O my soul, *zatoj sam tanka, džanum, rume-e-e-na*. Vuka runs as she'd run a good year ago through the stadium in her screamingly white new sneakers, runs and thinks of nothing, her mind numbed by fear, behind come racing the guys with glassy eyes and ravaged faces, she feels the breath of one on her left shoulder and hears the other's voice in her right ear, *Where do you think you're going to run*, he snarls, Vuka feels as if the runner was no longer her but a different Vuka, she's watching the whole scene from above and following, like a camera on a stalk, a young girl running from two scary guys, good thing she used to train, she thinks almost with satisfaction, but the guys are really fast too, as she realizes with bitterness, Vuka runs, the left-hand guy reaches for her bag, trying to rip it from her grasp, at first Vuka holds it tight but then lets it go, maybe then he'll leave her alone, but no, the ruffian slings the bag away, bounding after Vuka with even more zest, then the right-hand guy grabs Vuka by the jacket, Vuka somehow sheds it in her crazy flight, but the right-hand thug tosses the jacket on the ground and goes on running, Vuka is looking around for a *carabiniere* to turn to but there is none, people are walking past and noticing nothing, Vuka has no strength left to shout for help, she's simply trying to imagine the white stadium lines gliding by her feet, tears come sliding from her eyes and the wind is blowing them toward her ears, the left thug has almost grabbed her elbow, the right thug is pulling at the edge of her sweater, Vuka rises high high above the ROMA TERMINI sign, the subway noises subside, the train station din falls silent, below is running a small Vuka, as slowly as in a slow-motion picture, with the hands of both hoodlums reaching for her.

Tra-tam, tra-tam, the train wheels are rattling in the rhythm of a song which Vuka starts singing under her breath, *mene je majka dojila, džanum*, I was nursed by my mother, O my soul, *mene je majka, džanum, doji-i-i-la*, a song that surfaces in Vuka's mind on the Intercity train from Trieste to Rome. The landscape is rushing past her as if to elude her, and her neighbor's nodding head is drooping toward her left shoulder as if trying to slip away from its owner. Tra-tam, tra-tam, rattles the train to which she'd been accompanied by Mama, Papa, Vojo, and Aron, stubbornly pressing on through the landscape, just as she used to run as a little girl along the white lines painted on the stadium racetrack, so the train composition glides along the track of forking rails.

A black-dressed, angular lady with a red shawl enters the compartment, asking if the seat by the door is free. Sitting down, she gives Vuka a curious once-over as if she must have recognized a foreign accent, looking at her as if she knew about Vuka's innate difference. *She knows what it's all about*, Vuka reflects, leaning against the headrest to curb the embarrassment heating up her cheeks. *Good thing I know Italian*, she thinks to herself when the lady asks her where she's from. *From Yugoslavia*, says Vuka cheerfully, *from Sarajevo*. The lady wonders what it's like. *Lovely*, says Vuka, *my city's quite different from Rome, but lovely*, she adds, smiling at the memory of their Pelješac holiday, of how their neighbor kept lifting her brother Vojo by the ears to make him see Rome. But Italy no longer seems as fabulous as it did on holiday when they tried to glimpse it on the other side of the sea and she strained her eyes so long that she finally did seem to make out, just above the sea, the mountain skyline of a faraway land where princes and princesses walked and winged white horses flew.

With a drawn-out screech the Intercity stops at Florence, Vuka peers through the window and spots a stray dog roaming the platform, he looks like Vojo's shepherd dog. The train pulls out again, tra-tam, tra-tam, the wheels are rattling in the rhythm of the song which Vuka is singing under her breath, *zatoj sam tanka, visoka, džanum*, that's why I'm slender, tall, O my soul, *zatoj sam tanka, džanum, vis-o-o-o-ka. I'm going to Rome to take a course in Italian*, Vuka explains to the angular lady. Her fellow passenger's head painfully bumps against her gaunt shoulder, the man's eyelids, glued together, blink and he shifts his weight to the other side. The greenery is thickening into streaks brushing against the train, the trees and bushes are flashing past the window, sprinting as Vuka used to sprint along the left bank of the Miljacka River in the snow-white sneakers which are her pride.

Tickets, please, says the conductor, and all passengers in the compartment begin to rummage in their bags and pockets, Vuka's neighbor wakes up and glances around, bleary-eyed, *he's as cool as a cucumber*, Vuka thinks, *definitely not as ill at ease as me, he doesn't know the primal fear coursing through one's marrow.* Fear of people, of their words and acts, of whatever is to come, of the known and the unknown lurking in the future; fear of the presentiment of fear, of the question how it would be if all of this weren't here, if it were different, for better or worse. *What if a different dimension were to bring something terrible on her, what if a different destiny held a fairytale loveliness in store, then she really ought to go in terror of reality*, Vuka reflects, flooded with the primal fear of such predestinations.

The train arrives at an enormous railway station. Vuka waits for everyone to get off, then clambers from the train herself. The black-dressed lady with the red shawl says an icy goodbye. Vuka walks under the huge sign ROMA TERMINI, the terminus, the last stop, humming *zatoj sam tanka, rumena, džanum*, that's why I'm slender, rosy, O my soul, *zatoj sam tanka, džanum, rume-e-e-na*. Auntie Aga and her Italian husband will be waiting at the beginning of the platform.

Remington Noiseless

KAIROS, THE YOUNGEST OF Zeus's sons, anointed with olive oil, the one who has eluded the grasp of many, symbolizes the lucky moment which must be seized when the opportunity comes. My father's opportunity was the Turin World's Fair. To be sure, the showroom of Mr. Camillo Olivetti was more crowded, thanks to the new M1 model, but the salon of the American company for which father worked was besieged as well. Clear-cut letters, soft-touch keys, the maximum array and economy of symbols, four interlinear spaces, a decimal tab, elegant and practical shape—all that could be provided by just about anyone. But my father's trump card was that original birthright of letters: noiselessness. That was his Kairos's forelock, the only part by which Zeus's naked son could be caught.

With such machines, noiselessness refers not to silence but to respect for the typist's thought, the thought that shouldn't be disturbed by mechanic copying. In the 1930s, soon after father designed and produced for a large factory the masterpiece of his life, the Remington Noiseless typewriter, he returned to his native parts. It was in that year that I was born. I was not my father's masterpiece.

Don't touch those late 1930s Remingtons! They were made by strikebreakers! proclaimed the 1937 issue of *Consumers Union Reports*, a Philadelphia magazine, after trouble at the factory. Perhaps Father feared that his typewriter would never make it to the market, perhaps he sensed that the future lay not in silence but in the rattling of firearms, which were, in the torrent of rumors about possible war, manufactured with increasing zest by the American factory where he was employed at the time. And though the Remington Noiseless model was an instant success, our family was soon driven by Father's unknown fear to the land of his birth.

The weather in the south of Kvarner is fortunately less whimsical than in the northern part. In a town called Mali—The Little One, though it was larger than the others—we had a Venetian villa, and in a nearby bay a white hunting lodge with green shutters looking on the sea, where Father used to go hunting for pheasants. Never with a gun; he would set soundless nooses that would tighten around the bird's neck, suffocating it in an instant so that it never even had the time to squawk. I for my part was not interested in hunting, a ten-year-old, I ran around the coast with the island children, fighting victorious battles, winning princesses, and waging war for a large tract of the oak forest. Bruno, Stipe, Fulvia, and me were inseparable, strong Bruno, smart Stipe, blind Fulvia, a four-leaf band in those Bruno-Schulz-world summers, we outshouted the cicadas and the sun, the seagulls and clouds, we laughed throughout the summer, tricked the island creatures, cheated the confectioner of his caramels, tamed hedgehogs, stole octopus and cuttlefish from fishermen to dissect them, we enslaved the wind in our sails, drew eternal childhood from each season. The rain retreated from us, halting somewhere above the faraway mainland, which was beginning to thunder with the heavy cumuluses gathering over the bald pate of a choleric tyrant.

The war isolated both me and my family. Stipe and Bruno were no longer allowed to play with me, only Fulvia remained, whose blindness cleared up my thoughts and the prisms of falling rays. *What's the sea called in English*, she might ask. *Sea*, I told her. *Sea and see, the sea means to see*, she observed. She had the right answer to everything, the one you dimly envisage but can't coax out into the open. *What do you see if you look toward the sea*, I asked her. *The sea*, she replied. Blind Fulvia was my first love. I led her by the hand through the oak forest and olive groves, pressed little cypress cones into her palm and placed yellow palm blossoms behind her ears. We were alone, unwittingly members of a domineering nation, unwittingly members of a world which stretched far away from the island into space, that space of whose existence we wouldn't have even wanted to know. We belonged with the aggressors, the enemies, though we had harmed no one, and our friends would draw back when we walked along the town *riva*, and so passed the war, crouching almost silently somewhere in the distance.

My mother, an American, shrieked with despair when Father announced that it would be safer to meet and hopefully survive communism with our Trieste relatives. I, no expert at shrieking, forcefully clacked again and again in block capitals on the Remington that had been my fifteenth birthday present: NOT FAIR! I wanted that word on the ribbon to eclipse all I'd ever typed before. Father's laconic decisions couldn't be opposed, that much I knew. *You can't do this to us! It's enough, ti prego*, Mother begged him, faced with the third major move in her life. *Basta con le lagne, stop whining*, Father shut her down, *you have to seize the right moment*. If you want to raise a row and enforce your will at all costs, you have to do it in your own language or else keep silent in all languages, Father knew it well.

It has been gnawing at me ever since that I never gathered the courage to say goodbye to Fulvia, "goodbye" has always been a word that eclipsed for me all others.

After studying in Florence, I exported myself to France as a designer. I specialized in letter design, advertising boards, logos. I couldn't have managed it all without Laetitia. Accompanying me on my way forward and up, her willowy shadow kept me safe from the dazzling sun, which can burn you if you aren't careful.

At a Paris exhibition I saw a black-and-white photo by Lee Miller featuring a battered model of Father's typewriter, sitting in a dusty, bombed-out street among war ruins. *Remington Silent* was what the caption said.

*

Quiet, quiet, Father used to repeat at lunch, that's why I enjoy now the clatter of plates, twitter, nonsense platitudes that lighten up a meal. I like it when we chatter over each other as we did this summer, gathered again at the island hunting lodge which had passed to us with the Croatian restoration of private property after 1991. To hope for the restoration of our town villa as well would be too much. But I've always been satisfied with little, perhaps because my homeland has always been too big.

We're all here, Laetitia and our two sons, Jo and Philippe with his wife and adopted Indian children, Michael and Patrick, a miniature world in the Adriatic archipelago, a Tower of Babel among olive trees, we travel from language to language, from misunderstanding to misunderstanding. We're all here except for Father and Mother, who had since left Trieste only once in their lives, for heaven, earth or sea, wherever it is that we go at last: we're all here. Including Polka, an old English tracker, a piebald dachshund. She keeps me company in the boat and on forest paths, watches me filling thick paper *sacs d'environnement*, brought from France, with pine needles raked together in the fenced-off garden before our coastal house. The sandy beach was buried under gravel after World War II for sanitary reasons, eclipsing the yielding design of the past with a practical hardness, now it's a paradise for frolicking children and sluggish tourists. It's only toward the evening, with the beach grown empty and the sun growing red, that some of the locals will come strolling to the pier of the abandoned coast.

There she is, her hair turned gray, almost white, she comes several times a week, muttering incomprehensible words to herself, surrounded by five grandchildren who are chasing each other and jumping into the water, five fair-haired offspring of a grandmother who used to be as dark as the ink of a Remington ribbon. *Fulvia*, I called to her when I first saw her this summer. She peered at me mistrustfully, cocking her head in disbelief, and went on absently muttering her mantra-like litanies.

The clouds in their inimitable font are obscuring the steely horizon. It occurred to me that Fulvia had sat on her hometown pier throughout my stay in Trieste and later in France, muttering under her breath Circe's spells, come lull or gale.

Polka, maison, I called, *Polka, home!* Poor dog, she doesn't even know where home is, is it the noisy Paris apartment or the quiet hunting lodge on the island, we've been tossing her around the world like a parcel with a misspelled address. When she and we wanderers are gone, perhaps a cenotaph will be erected for us on no-man's coast. It will bear the silent typing: HERE REST THE SAILORS WHO WERE DRIVEN BY WINDS ALL OVER THE COMPASS ROSE.

Out of Oblivia

WHILE WE WERE LEARNING about Simón Bolívar in today's history class, I thought about Hanna. Hanna had stayed at home, most likely she's still going to our old school and probably still wearing her gray school uniform. Mine is blue now, the color of my eyes. I stand out in my class because I'm blond, too. All the people here have a dark complexion and black hair and are somehow like each other, definitely more so than we were at home. I asked Grandma-Abuela why and Grandma-Abuela answered, *Other places, other customs.* My grandma knows a lot but won't tell much. I like her because she's so mysterious.

Our history teacher knows a lot and tells us a lot, too. I like her as well. Bolivia is named for Simón Bolívar, he is *El Libertador*, so she explained. At home we had to memorize the saying *Si de Rómulo Roma, de Bolívar Bolivia*, if the name *Rome* comes from Romulus, Bolivia is named for Simón Bolívar.

In my spare time I sometimes browse through our Leica photos, and the photos show me what it was like at home. The grandest of all is the picture of Daddy-Papá wearing a military cap, the cap of an important soldier. That cap imbued him with courage and pride. I don't know what he's properly called, an important soldier like that, because I'm only ten. There's our old residence in the photo as well. It's funny that *residencia* means only *home* here. Mamá says that words which are the same in several languages but mean different things are called false friends. A funny name. It occurred to me once that Hanna might be a false friend, too, because she never wrote back.

Our school went on an escursion, or excursion, to La Paz. La Paz is the highest capital in the world. What I remember best is the witch market. I don't believe in such things anymore and neither does my classmate, Juanita Leal. Juanita says that there are no miracles. On the stalls of the La Paz witch market we saw dried frogs and unborn llamas and figurines to chase evil spirits away, and we listened to the locals playing the charanga. The vendors chatted in Quechua, but I don't understand it. Lots of people here speak Quechua, my classmates included, but Spanish is trouble enough for me. We speak Spanish at home, too. Daddy-Papá says it's better and in fact the right thing to do. Because we're not Spaniards and we're making a lot of mistakes in Spanish, it's not just us who are learning Spanish but Spanish is practicing on us, too. It was harder for Daddy-Papá and Mamá to learn the language, and Grandma-Abuela still says this and that the way we do, for instance, she's often repeating the counting-out rhyme *I and you, miller's cow, miller's donkey, that is you.*

Grandma-Abuela cries a lot but only in secret. Sometimes I hear her clinking with her *mate* cup at night and sobbing in her room, but I don't dare to go to her because I'm officially supposed to be sleeping. Grandma-Abuela, who's hard of hearing to boot, says that we had to come to Bolivia because our home country had been taken over by bad guys, but some day we'll return and get back our things which were much prettier than here. Our things must be missing us. At home I had haircombs carved from ivory, a porcelain doll, and a mirror frame set with color gems, but here all things have more or less the same Indian pattern. At home we had fine furniture and two cars but here we live in an ordinary house with spiny agaves in the yard and we've got an old jalopy, as Mamá says.

Daddy-Papá and Mamá are quarreling much more. Once I begged them that we might return home, *por favor*, where everything was prettier and easier. And I could ask Hanna why she never wrote back. But Daddy-Papá and Mamá kept quiet and never answered. That's bothering me.

Once Juanita Leal and her family invited me on a several days' trip to Argentina, to Villa General Belgrano, a town like our own towns, with wooden beams on house fronts and sloping roofs and begonias in the windows, there are supposed to be a lot of inns flowing with German beer. But Daddy-Papá wouldn't hear of it, though I told him that I'd certainly feel better in such a town because ours used to look like that. I daresay the town would be happy to host me, too. A person can hardly believe it: you can be born in one part of the world, but when you move across a big sea, everything changes. Only the stars look the same on a clear night.

I know about gravity, the attractive force coming from the center of the Earth, which makes my blanket fall to the floor in Bolivia just as it used to fall from my home bed. Even if there's a big sea in between. All over the world, children's blankets fall to the floor, even when their country happens to be on the lower side of the globe that night; rather than float downward into space, the blanket drops on the floor because the children are closer to the red-hot core of our planet than to the sky. I'm glad of it because it means that there's some order on our Earth in spite of all the migrations.

Otherwise I'm allowed to go play at Juanita's any time. Sometimes we study together. I'm good at history. I like history and I hope it likes me, too. I helped Juanita when our teacher, Javier, told us about Ulysses and we had to write summaries of his adventures. For me, his strangest adventure was the one where his companions ate lotus blossoms in the land of the Lotophagi, which made them forget not only their homeland and families but even their language. Trying to articulate the most basic words they'd known since childhood, they simply drooled plant juice. I summarized this episode for homework and Teacher Javier told me I'd done a good job, except that I'd made some orthography mistakes. It wasn't me who made them, really, they intruded on their own.

One time our bell was rung by a colorful poncho and a man's hat. The poncho and hat enclosed an Indian woman. She began to tell us something in Quechua but we didn't understand. Daddy-Papá drove her away quite brusquely and she retorted *sajgra!* as if she were calling down on us a native curse.

Anyway, Daddy-Papá can't stand visitors at all. For this purpose he's had a windowless cabinet built in the center of our one-story house. Its only connection to the other rooms is the door. There he listens to Mozart, Beethoven, and Haydn because he says it's the only room where the sound is pure, untainted by street noise. Only there can he listen to German music and utter pure words. Though most of the time he keeps silent even there.

Sometimes Daddy-Papá sort of loses his marbles and rummages through every nook and cranny, searching behind shelves and cupboards and in the cellar, once he wanted to demolish the living room wall, another time he took apart our black phone. He's afraid of bugs we never had at home. They can even be hiding under the surfaces of our stuff, they can crawl into the inmost crannies of our things and our house. They're called *micrófonos*, that's their Bolivian, or rather Spanish, name because there's no such thing as the Bolivian language. *Micrófonos* are tiny with a metallic black gleam, like the beetles that leak a stinking liquid if you squash them. Daddy-Papá thought he'd found one. They're very tough, so he jumped up and down on it to crack it.

Mamá believes it's this varmint that's making Daddy-Papá act strange. I don't see how such a tiny thing can get on your case. As long as your blanket lands on the floor at night, even at the end of the world, it means that everything is all right. And luckily I can always find shelter in Grandma-Abuela's arms. I comfort us both by saying that she couldn't be a grandma at all if it weren't for me. Grandma-Abuela is hard of hearing, at least that's what she lets on, so she can live in the world as it was before we moved here to Bolivia. She can pretend that she's forgotten the new world and only remembers the old one. That's what I call forgetting from the back. Sometimes I ask her, *Grandma-Abuela, tell me how it was . . .* And at such times Grandma-Abuela hears perfectly well and tells me all in detail: what our home looked like, what we cooked, what she chatted about with her women friends at Thursday meetings, what it was like when I was born. And about Grandpa—while he was still alive, of course; I've only a vague memory of him. But she never talks about our last weeks at home when we had to pack up in a panic and travel here. That's something Grandma-Abuela no longer remembers.

I've heard that when one of their relatives dies, the natives no longer talk about him. They never pronounce his name again, and if the name happens to mean dawn, wave, or peace, these words refuse to be used ever again in everyday conversation. They have to be replaced by others. Grandma-Abuela, though, does mention Grandpa from time to time.

Sometimes I daydream about someone fitting our roof back home with hooks on a wire, then transporting it here by plane. Or the other way round, about transporting the Bolivian house back home. I don't believe in miracles anymore, though, no more than Juanita does. I'm just hoping we'll go back soon. If I don't step on a crack on my way from school, that means we're going back. Eva believes it, too. Eva, that's my doll. She has a gray tartan skirt and a red apron. Whenever I wash the apron, it bleeds the color red, leaving blood-tinted droplets in the sink, just like that time at home when Daddy-Papá didn't clean up well after himself when he came from work at night and rinsed his boots and uniform. In the morning I went to the bathroom and the pink drops hadn't dried yet, they even dotted the ceramic tiles on the wall. Mamá hurried to wipe them away. I remember her foot striking against a bottle under the sink.

Whenever I'm blue in the evening, partly because Hanna never writes back, Mamá tells me that we can't return because we wouldn't be free at home anymore, something we're supposed to be here. It reminds me of a cartoon joke I saw in a Saturday paper: aquarium fish were saying about the humans on the other side of the glass pane, *Oh, poor things, cooped up all their lives on the other side!* Perhaps I think that Hanna is imprisoned and I'm free, while she thinks exactly the opposite.

I'm pondering all this now when I have a fever every four days and must drink a very bitter medicine. This sickness attacks you when you've been bitten by a mosquito, but I'm sure it's the fault of the bugs in the house, those *micrófonos*. And I'm very sad, not only because I can't go to school where I'm doing well. I'm not sad only because I don't get to see my friend, Juanita Leal, and because crying wrings tears from Grandma-Abuela's eyes at night. Just before I fell sick I saw my father tearing to pieces a white envelope with a red and blue border. It bore Hanna's name, her address, and the phrase *PAR AVION*. I knew what stood on the envelope. I'd written the letter myself and asked my mother to mail it. Stupid letter, why did it allow itself to be torn to shreds!

Last night I dreamed that Christopher Columbus wrote a letter to the Spanish queen on arriving in America, but what ended up in her hands was only half of the written page, ripped away by the tempest. The queen assumed that Columbus hadn't arrived anywhere but was still roaming the great sea.

It's dark and I think that the fourth day is coming, the day of the growing fever. My pajamas are damp through and through and sweat is pouring down my forehead. At first I felt really hot but now I'm shaking with the cold. I hear someone calling for me, outside. A blanket enfolds me and I rise from the bed, almost falling down, my legs refusing to carry me. When I step out, there's a large basket sitting in front of the house, with a gaudy balloon floating above in Indian patterns and colors. Boarding the basket are Daddy-Papá, Mamá, and Grandma-Abuela, Juanita is shouting happily, *My folks are letting me go with you!* and in Teacher Javier's palm there's fluttering a white handkerchief embroidered with Ulysses's ship. I too clamber into the basket, simply in my pajamas, and the balloon begins to rise. Grandma-Abuela says, *I'll have to forget again.* Suddenly there's a bang and a puff of smoke, there's Simón Bolívar standing below and shooting a ceremonial salute in the air. I'm hoping that our one-story house, which is traveling with us, doesn't crash on him and that the shots of the rapidly shrinking man haven't pierced the balloon canvas. Bolivia is turning into a dotted fairytale landscape, if there ever was such a land at all.

Jet Lag

THE BEST THING ABOUT hovering is that you never know where you are, but at least once in your life you know where you're coming from and where you're going, or, in this case, where you took wing and where you're flying. Wallowing in this certainty you're asked by the stewardess if you would like anything to drink, she offers you two beverages in three languages with an affable smile, while your winged guardian, seated on the other side of the plane, is eyeing you morosely above today's issue of *Pravda*.

If you sharply glance over your shoulder, peering through the porthole back to the east, you can see the sun mocking the airplane's butt, you find yourself high up, like a satellite that circles around the Earth erasing meridians, piercing the atmosphere, you're making your way straight west, to the place where the sun will finally outwit you in this game of chase by delaying the hours, even though it will set too early.

One night three of them came pounding on my door, and when I opened, they said, *Comrade Iosif Alexandrovich, you're coming with us.* First they took me to the commissariat, where a grave gentleman in a threadbare jacket pressed into the hand of my secret guardian angel all required papers and two airplane tickets, and two hours later we were already waiting at the Leningrad airport, Shosseynaya. I might say that men of darkness wanted to banish me into light, but the light turned out to be a life replacement rather than a sunbath.

From the cramped institution where tongues were being hacked off, I came into the freedom of a sinking civilization, from the Arkhangelsk prison, where they would wrap me in cold wet sheets in winter, I came into the electrified embrace of a synthetic blanket. First to Imperial Vienna, then further. At Heathrow I was picked up by English poets, my beloved Auden among them, who arranged a new existence for me, existence, not life, life had been that earlier phase with all its thorns, stumblings, and unstoppable blood.

My homeland cast her veins and arteries like a fishing net all over the continent and, laughing, reeled in the scanty catch. I'll only feel safe on the other side of the Atlantic, I mused and took a seat on another airplane, *Would you like anything to drink?* asked the stewardess, offering me seven beverages in a single master language, I asked for a coffee and stayed awake till I died, insomnia seized my rhymes, rhythm, and meter.

A Russian poet of Jewish origin, an English essayist and American citizen: as if I had remained forever hovering above the Atlantic, on top of a Venetian bridge which spanned a canal flowing with human liquids, iambic hendecasyllables and cold echoes, suspended between the original and the search for an equivalent which should be, as in translating, no mere replacement.

My story isn't pleasurable, my story is no adventure from the iconography of good and evil continents and steel curtains: read no more. My story is the story of a man who was exiled from his homeland only to come home, from the ambiguity of guilt into a precise mechanism with cogs and wheels that could grind one to golden dust. A mechanism with a single spoke in its wheels: my translating.

Russia wouldn't have me, I was labeled a parasite of society and asked during my trial who had given me the right to proclaim myself a poet. Had I perhaps finished a poet's school, poet's university, poet's apprenticeship? Then I was sent up north, to prisons, to Kresty and to Norenskaya village, classified in my papers as a schizophrenic. And how true it was, except that I've only become a schizophrenic now, torn between two worlds in an eternal jet lag.

The news of my trial became public knowledge and spread abroad, an international scandal broke out and I had to be ditched elegantly, they sent a winged guardian to escort me on the plane and fly me to Vienna, the city where scum were deposited and left to scatter all over the planet.

There the winged one abandoned me, or rather seemed to, in truth he still spied on me and even traveled to New York, where he would sneak into my room at night to rub my tongue with emery paper, in the morning the floor by my bed would be littered with shavings and white whittlings would curl from the muscle in my mouth. I was uprooted and, as I've written in a poem, I've never since put a question mark after the words *where to.*

Marina Vasilyevna, whom I had left in Leningrad, now St. Petersburg, sent me letters to America, she knew what had happened to me, that I had not left of my own free will but had been exiled instead, she wrote me crystal-clear letters from which I learned my language all over again. I had not left her alone, I had left her with a promise and an unborn child, *We'll make it somehow, the two of us,* I told her on the left bank of the Karpovka when we last saw each other, we were standing in front of the conservatory, which was mirrored in the canal and resounded with a Renaissance vocal duet, *the three of us,* I corrected myself although I knew that she would never be allowed out of the country, or I back in.

In America I continued to write, and as I trusted no one, I translated my poems into English myself. I was discovering new tones, words, and meanings unknown to Anglo-Saxons, I was combining elements into nonexistent sentences, they said, *We don't get this,* they said, *The guy doesn't even know English,* they said, *Now what sort of experiment is this?* They couldn't interpret what I had served them still warm under the lid of their sky, they were ungrateful, they were like Soviet censorship, they couldn't understand my feeling of guilt at betraying my language with theirs. Just as I betrayed Marina Vasilyevna, whom, as I foresaw, I was never to see again.

Angela understood that those translations of my poems were not my choice but simply dictated by the verses, she enfolded me, Angela, she covered my fluffy pastry dough like exotic icing. I was faithful to them, to my American Angela and to Russian poetry, they were a refuge, arms open wide, the scent of home, *You coming over, I hug you, let's go movies tonight*, she said in the painstaking speech of an unassimilated person. *You look like Michael Caine*, she said on our third date and kissed my reciter's lips, from which issued new words built from Russian frame and English clay. *Now what sort of experiment is this?* they said. Only Angela knew what I was saying, we communicated like two squawking seagulls.

Auden understood me, too, he said I was like Icarus in Brueghel's picture, falling while the plowman and shepherd are looking away. The plummeting boy, his leg still sticking out of the sea, is overlooked even by the ship calmly sailing by, his disaster unnoticed. *Of course, I'm not Icarus but Daedalus*, I wisecracked, *I've managed to fly by the sun on unmelted wings*. But we both knew that he was right. Besides, Brueghel's Icarus looks boyishly awkward, like an urchin trying to show off an impossible leap and crashing on the ground, that's how I must have looked with my idiolectal inventions in another language, they thought I was awkward but in fact I simply hadn't managed to translate what I wanted to say in Russian, so I thought that a new glittering costume might infuse my original lines with a fresh charm.

After a long interval, the winged one perched down on my bed again one sleepless night and shook me by the shoulder.

He had the Brezhnew-style eyebrows of Czesław Miłosz and a kindly voice, hardly typical of winged people in general. *Dear Osya*, he said, *the woman sleeping by your side is dreaming about loud canyons, fertile prairies and Indian summers, never about jejune steppes.* I glanced mistrustfully at sleeping Angela, peacefully roaming through her dream landscapes.

The next day I took her to Block Island. *I give you this island as a gift*, I told her, *because it's as sharp and simple as you are.* This was the touchstone; if she accepts it, she is mine to the last fiber, if she hesitates, she is like a secret police official, suspiciously examining the note. *Personal characteristics: schizophrenic.* The wind was lifting her scarf as she answered, *On this island you're king and I'm queen, we're tyrants and everything must be done as we command, the islanders may eat nothing but fish and talk only in the fish dialect.* Clearly, the winged one had been wrong, wanting to plant a seed of doubt in me, Angela is mine despite the ocean which cleaves the world in two, we can communicate in fish speech, what matters is that everything has its form, in form lies the freedom of the world. I took a picture of her to preserve that moment forever, the Polaroid photo oozed out of the camera and Angela's face in it was obscured by the hand of the winged one, who reached for the photo at that very instant, snatching it from my sight before I could take a proper look at it. Angela was laughing as if she saw nothing, I glanced around in alarm, while the winged one was by now only a faraway grinning speck.

If truth be told, he didn't fly but sooner ran or fled, hovering above the ground. Since I'd always considered flying or winged creatures in literature kitschy, I forbore from dashing after him. Just let him hurry, let him wear down his footsoles, let him fray his feathers, he, too, is doomed to oblivion despite the photo in his hands. *And what's the point of forgetting if it's followed by dying?* shouted the winged one from the distance, *paste that to the end of some poem and it'll be remembered forever*, he grinned.

Only then did I notice that the winged one had the mouth of

Marina Vasilyevna—that it was she who was speaking. *Marina Vasilyevna!* I shouted, and Marina Vasilyevna stepped up to me, she faced me there on Block Island like a character from *The Invention of Morel.* I reached for her to make sure that she was real, *You'll never pull it off,* she said, *even if you were to run through all thirteen time zones separating New York from St. Petersburg, you'd still lag behind, there's lead in your feet, never again can you catch up with me, never can you make up for that time, all is lost. I've given birth to your son, he'll grow up fatherless and you'll grow old childless, the two of you out of synch forever.*

I stood there with Angela's hand in mine, Marina Vasilyevna vanished in the hot air like a water mirage, and in the crowd of people carrying baskets of lemons or olives on their shoulders, I, like Bruno in my friend's poem, couldn't find the word farewell for her either in Russian or in English. I envisioned myself sitting on an airplane with unmeltable wings, chasing after the winged Marina Vasilyevna and returning, amid the stewardess's offers of three beverages in two languages, eastward through the languages of all thirteen time zones between New York and St. Petersburg, with departure this morning and possible arrival this evening, eternally lagging behind the world.

The Feud

SLATE COVERED HOUSES ARE tossing to each other the echo of my heels against the dark pavement, the dazzle of the sun is painting the chiaroscuro of the afternoon, and for a moment I'm enveloped by deafening fly buzz in the scorchingly fresh silence. Penta di Casinca, the prettiest village in the world, was mine that summer, and that August, as scarlet as the voice of my instrument, was mine too. I claim them for my own, Penta and that month, just as God may claim the world.

Why not practice at my weekend cottage in Corsica, suggested Professor Fernando, *you'll have peace there.* He was really kind, a proper altruist with no hidden interests lurking in the background, anyone who knew him could confirm it. I met him at a violin summer school in Aix and complained at the farewell dinner how I'd love to stay in France a month longer but couldn't possibly practice in hotels or pensions. The next day he turned up in front of the changing room, dangling his key between thumb and index finger, smiling. *Go as soon as you can, while it's still summer,* he encouraged me, and the very next day I embarked on a boat for Bastia.

I decided on a counterclockwise route, or the whole thing might have been too simple: a godsent offer, my destination reached on the very next day—no, no way. Having rented a car at Bastia, I drove across high, barren hills to the west coast and followed it down south. Algajola, Calvi, Calanche, Cargèse, Ajaccio, seaside tourist resorts, bullet-pierced bilingual signs, "CORSICA LIBERA," then a suicidal road with the verge crumbling into chasms; coves lined with red rocks deep below, as if you could catch a glimpse of that beauty only by getting yourself killed; skinny cows that came sauntering around a blind curve; shepherd cottages and shepherds who would scowl if you came too close to their starving flocks; and then again, as if you were in another country, luxurious yachts at picturesque Bonifacio with its dazzling white fortress, built on a cliff which literally overhangs the sea. From this extreme southern tip I traveled up the east side, climbing steeply toward the north, driving along a boring, straight sandy coast. Menhirs, the former Corsican capital of Aleria, aloes and cactuses, agaves, eucalyptus trees, the plain and the steep slopes rising above its heart, I turned left and climbed up a narrow road to the mountain village which I would soon adopt for my own.

Even as I got out, everything in me quieted down, I felt my heart begin to beat as it always should beat. Ferrando's house was not hard to find, standing in the middle of the main street—the only proper street, in fact, not counting the few perpendicular lanes. Penta, although a village, gave the impression of a country town, the old dark houses were nearly genteel though not all in the best condition, and the grandest of them was beyond doubt the former town hall, concealed behind a showy oleander.

The Professor's house was narrow, rising to two stories and modestly furnished, which was fine with me: bed, wardrobe, table, cupboard, shelves, bathroom. But I felt driven out, into fresh air, I had to buy food and drink anyway. I crisscrossed Penta but there was no store or bar, let alone an inn, I would have to drive to the nearest settlement in the valley. Whenever I went out in those early days, I only heard the clatter of plates from a few houses, the rest seemed deserted. Well, at least I would disturb nobody: after all, I had to polish Stamitz's *Concerto in D Major for Viola and Orchestra*. So my first days passed in practice and lonely walks through the ghost village, I barely met a living soul except sometimes a local woman, Anne, with whom I exchanged a few words, and once a couple of tourists. *Very few inhabitants are left here, lots of houses are empty but you're lucky to have a neighbor, in the house leaning against yours lives Pierre, a retired colonel, he's a pied noir, which means an Algerian Frenchman, he used to live down there but now he's very old and frail,* Anne told me. Ever since I heard of him, I divined rather than felt his presence, a health worker was said to drive up from the valley every Monday to tend to him, but I had never seen her yet.

Some days later, however, our neighborliness became more tangible, for whenever I drew my bow across the strings, I would hear knocks from the other side of the wall, knock knock, which soon gained in strength, thud thud, and ended in incomprehensible shouting. With all those empty houses out there, of course it had to be the one bordering on mine that was lived in, with such peace here, a musician's dream, I had to stumble on that rarity, an old man with sharp hearing. I might have callously ignored the manias of the old colonel, who had presumably raised his share of Cain with cannon fire and banging rifles in his day, but I couldn't, I had never disturbed a soul, I'd always practiced at the music academy and rarely at home, and even then by agreement with the neighbors just from ten to noon, period.

Should I call at his house and work out a schedule with him as well, a time when I wouldn't disturb him, should I explain that my instrument was special, no violin and no ordinary viola either but a viola d'amore with a scarlet voice? But then I'd never seen him at all, he'd never stuck his nose out of the house since I arrived.

In spite of my principles I decided that this time, the only time in my life, I would break my rule and ruthlessly put myself and my instrument first. Knock knock knock, it rang out as I began to play, thud thud thud, it continued, to be followed by a raised voice. This recurred for five days but I doggedly practiced on, merely replacing Stamitz with Vivaldi once: the old colonel's response was the same. I found it hard to concentrate and was unsettled by his pummeling against the wall, who does he think he is, does he take me for one of his soldiers, ordering me around like that? *If only he'd fall quiet*, I wished from the bottom of my heart—I ought to hone the piece to perfection if such a thing existed at all, because a solo concert was awaiting me in October.

On the seventh day the old man no longer made a sound. Again the village was enveloped in silence, broken only by the singing of birds and the buzzing of insects, again it was mine and my heartbeat slowed down to what it had been at my arrival. Again I was alone, even the hint of an annoying neighbor had been scattered. Yes, again I was alone, all too lonesome, even lonely. Time had stopped, and I with it. The singing of my viola echoed through the village, hardening into timelessness, we three were hovering in immateriality, Penta di Casinca, my instrument and me, and I felt that I could become the mistress of this wordless infinity, I, the only shipwrecked survivor of this soundless boundlessness. Anything I made up could come true, there was nothing and no one to gainsay it, and so I met Nadjad, *I'm half-French, half-Kabyle*, he said on introducing himself, *that is, half-Berber, I live in Paris and lecture on anthropology, but I've come to Corsica to study blood feud, a very popular way of settling scores up to the mid-nineteenth century*. Our first encounter at the end of the village, where the gaze dropped to the green lowlands, was bathed in the setting sun. *At this hour life in my native town begins to die down*, said Nadjad, *it grows dark, the curfew approaches both in the kasbah and the European district.—Tell me about your places*, I asked him the next day, when we were already on *tu* terms. *Azul-N-Gerger*, he said, *azul'n gerger*, I repeated, *Azul-N-Ain-El-Hammam, Azul-N-Bgayet*, he continued, *azul'n bgayet*, I articulated: this was easier.

Indeed, ever since Nadjad came, all had been possible, all feasible, I just had to wish for it. *I'm so calm here*, I confessed to him, *I've never been so calm before.* "Our heart is restless until it finds its rest in thee," *this is what St. Augustine said, a Berber on his father's side like me.* But it seemed that true peace had only settled within me now, with Nadjad's arrival at Penta. *I don't know anything about these things,* I admitted, *or about St. Augustine.—He immersed himself in the problem of evil,* continued Nadjad, in fact, *he started as a Manichean. Evil was the absence of God, so he claimed, and had no existence of its own. The world was good while evil was produced by human disobedience. Human disobedience,* the words kept ringing in my ears and I tried to chase the annoying phrase away, at Penta we all seemed beyond laws, human or divine.

Tell me something about blood feud instead, I asked him at lunch at my, that is to say, Ferrando's, place. *It was honorable brigandry, and an honorable brigand had to go into hiding after committing a crime,* he explained, *so their number was limited, though the phenomenon had been widespread two centuries ago. The best-known honorable brigands were the brothers Bellacoscia, Nicolaï, Castelli, Romanetti and so on, but why should I bore you with this, listen to this music instead,* said Nadjad, inserting a cassette in my radio. From the box came floating modern Oriental music, *Hamid Idir, a Kabyle singer and songwriter,* Nadjad explained, laughing.

So we might spend our days at Penta, Nadjad and me, as long as possible, until the end of time. And the next morning he'd bring me coffee to bed and stroke my hair. *What shall we do today?* he'd ask, and I'd suggest we might go back to the end of the village, under the thick-spreading tree, to the vantage point which commanded a view of the lowlands all the way to the sea. *Tranquility, there's such tranquility here,* he said, almost making me laugh at the word, *there's none in Paris or Algiers. Once I was attacked in the Bab El Ued quarter and my legs buckled under me so that I could neither stand nor run, I just collapsed onto the curb, at such times all your principles fail, all your grand ideas topple to the pavement together with you.* Then he told me about the circumstances in Algeria, the Muslim extremists who were killing Berbers and Arab intellectuals, seventy murdered foreigners who had dared to cling on to the country even after the fundamentalist threat, he told me about the FIS and GIA organizations, the assassinations on the former President, Muhammad Boudiaf, and Prime Minister Kasdi Merbah, a bomb attack which claimed child victims, about murdered journalists, about killing.

Clouds gathered over Penta, rain came pouring down and we took refuge in Ferrando's house. When I came from the bathroom where I had dried my hair and changed, he was raptly gazing through the window and crooning to himself. *Mon pays est une rose, ils l'ont dépouillée de ses pétales, Oh, a pop song by Cheb Rabah,* he said, embarrassed, *you can't be interested in this kind of thing, tell me about your instrument instead.—The viola, viola d'amore, would you like to hear it,* I perked up to hear him show an interest in it at last. *It's a quint lower than a violin, I always say that it has a scarlet voice.* He wondered why it was called d'amore: *I'll play it for you, you'll see at once.*

I struggled with all my might to make my dream obey me, but when I woke the next morning, I saw him reading an Arab paper. *Is this supposed to be read from back to front?* I asked, laughing, but he was in no mood for jokes, *Rashid Mimouni died in Paris, an Algerian writer who condemned fundamentalism,* he said grimly and laid the paper, *El Vatan,* aside. Now and then my dreams would break loose, with harsh reality waiting to displace them, but I wouldn't slacken my hold, I did struggle with all my strength to make my imagination obey me.

I wished that time might harden into slate and Nadjad stay with me at Penta forever. That our talks might never wind down and our walks never end, that he might tell me, *How lucky I am to have met you, you're my alibi for this fathomlessness and I'm your alibi for the timelessness.* That he might tell me what he heard when I played the viola, instead of always harping on hapless Algeria, on the Berbers and the wrongs committed against them, on how they sympathized with their French colonists in contrast to Algerian Arabs. That he'd never have told me the story of his mother who was not a Kabyle but an Arab, killed by a French colonel.

It was days later that it dawned on me at last. A French colonel in Algeria and a murdered Arab mother. I walked over to the house supposedly rented by Nadjad, but there was no trace of him, the door stood closed and mute. Colonel Pierre, goodness, he hadn't let out a peep for a week, it was true I had been practicing less since Nadjad arrived (as he claimed), but still, the other side of the wall lay quiet. I went to the only local I had spoken to over the last fortnight, *Anne*, I asked, *do you know where Nadjad is, the Berber tourist from Paris?* and Anne shook her head, *I've never seen him*, she said. I returned to Ferrando's house, my thoughts darting to and fro as if they had snapped from benumbed slumber, goodness, tomorrow is Monday, the health worker is coming to check on the colonel, she'll see what happened, call the police. Nadjad hasn't been seen by anyone, he is clean, but me, what will happen to me, the one who should have been my alibi is gone. I knew in an instant what I would do. Pack my things into my suitcase, clean up after myself meticulously, wipe off my fingerprints as well, particularly those in the colonel's house, and take the first boat to the mainland.

For the last time, the slate covered houses are tossing to each other the echo of my heels against the dark pavement, the dazzle of the sun is painting the chiaroscuro of the afternoon, and for a moment I'm enveloped by deafening fly buzz in the scorchingly fresh silence. Penta di Casinca, the prettiest village in the world, was mine that summer, and that August, as scarlet as the voice of my instrument, was mine too. I claim them for my own, Penta and that month, just as God may claim the world.

I'm the demiurge of my dreams, and Nadjad will go on living in them. *Augustine quotes Paul's letter to the Romans,* my friend will say as we're watching from the boat the white foam on blue water: O man, who art thou that repliest against God? Hath not the potter power over the clay, of the same lump to make one vessel unto honor, and another unto dishonor?

Olivija

EVERYTHING HAS BEEN DIFFERENT since we came to Sarajevo. Milk is different, bread tastes different, coffee is called *kahva* and isn't like ours at all, it has tiny grains that stick to the tongue even after you've drunk it up, but only if you've tipped too hard the little handleless cup called a *fildžan*. Once you learn to drink Turkish coffee, you can even tell fortunes from the grounds, and a Serbian writer said that drinking coffee in Bosnia was close to divinity because you sat down at God's feet: the coffee grounds held the future and if you drank such coffee, you'd blended the past, present, and future. *If you drank coffee without grounds, you only lived in the present,* so he said.

There are things that have more or less the same names everywhere, but the names here are totally different: a diamond is *almas*, a sofa is *minder*, an angel is *melek*. We bring new words from the store where the shop assistant, despite her reasonable grasp of English, teaches us her language with a professorial determination, she says *šećer*, for instance, and won't let us go until we've repeated it with the *ch* as palatal and palatable as Turkish Delight, even if we've already paid. New words are brought home by Keira, too, though her school is international; she tells me about the local singers, imitating their singing with a peculiar articulation of the letter *l* in which the tongue is raised to the palate and teeth.

It's only at work, in a modern building downtown, that I find myself in an environment more like ours. Metal desks, neon lights, and cables running over the floor, but as soon as

I turn on my computer, I'm flooded by the whole of Bosnia, all the martyrdom, all the riddles. At first my screen flashes the logo ICMP and I have to type three secret passwords to open the program and access confidential files. Archived files are even secured with three additional passwords, like the case of nine-year-old Mustafa R. My daughter Keira is nine, too, and ever since I learned about the Mustafa R. case, I've shuddered whenever Keira touches my makeup in the bathroom.

Coming home from work, I'm always wiped out, but thankfully Lucas has hot dinner waiting for me. We eat and talk, Keira tells me about school and as I listen, I admire her maturity because she pretends to like it here even though I know that she misses her old home school. After our early dinner I sit down together with Keira, helping her with her homework; this time she has to write a composition about her parents' work and profession. *I work for the ICMP*, I tell her, *that's short for the International Commission on Missing Persons.*

Why are they missing? Keira wants to know.

Because there was a war here twenty years ago and a lot of people got lost.

And you guys are finding them?

Not all of them.

Do you bring them home?

Not all, some of them are dead, I'm blunt.

So why do you look for them if they're dead?

To restore their names to them, I say.

Did they lose their names, too? she asks.

A name is another word for identity, something Keira wouldn't understand. The identities of people, of butchered corpses and body parts can be restored through the DNA analysis of their hair, nails, blood.

As I don't answer, she goes on: *Did they lose one of those weird names like* baklava *or* kuća *for a house? You could give them other names, new. I'd like Jenny better.*

It's the same as with Olivija, I answer.

Days ago, Lucas noticed something moving in a vase where we rarely changed water. Hurrying to the windowsill with a glass jar that houses a bamboo stalk, Keira and I saw a tiny creature. *It's a tadpole*, I said, *and when it grows up it will turn into a frog, climb up the bamboo stalk, and hop out. I'm not having this at home.*

Lucas and Keira exchanged conspiratorial glances as only a father and daughter can. *But, Mom . . .*

I'd always had a horror of small slimy creatures but I could have put up with a frog. In a few days, however, the creature began to develop differently than displayed on the Internet, stretching out like a water worm. What might it develop into? A writhing snake or a European alligator variant, a tiny mutant crocodile? But before I even got round to protesting, the creature got a name.

She'll be called Olivija, with a "j" as they'd spell it here, she's a native after all, Keira decided, and before I could remonstrate, Lucas was already smiling appreciatively.

Why just Olivija? Why not Esma, Azra, or Aga? When something or someone, even the paltriest of creatures, receives a name, they enter a different sphere. A name means feeling. *Adolf* freezes people's blood, *Michelangelo* takes their breath away, *Jesus* sparks off clashing opinions and passions, an anonymous corpse viewed in the flesh can never shake you as deeply as a photo showing the mauled body of Hazemina Islamić, Enes Pahirspahić, or Bekrija Osmanić. Our name is the vessel of our essence, we stand or fall with it. Naming our child, we pour into the name all our love, and with that name she'll live out her time, she'll have to defend and guard it to make others respect it.

You can't simply get rid of a creature from the vase once it has been named, all you can do with a named creature is grow attached to it and start loving it. You savor Bosnian *kahva* with more relish than ordinary coffee despite the ground grains straying under your tongue, and when you say *baklava*, you catch an unconscious whiff of walnuts and honey. That's what a name does.

Our name is us, though my work here at the missing war victims center requires that sixty percent of a skeleton should be found if the person's identity and full name are to be restored one hundred percent. Without help from the victims' relatives we couldn't establish much, it's them who provide the materials for name searching. Rather than with the aid of letters, their names are established through the—currently—90,000 blood samples and 150,000 filed biological samples. We've excavated 3,000 mass burial sites and restored names to 18,000 people. Their names aren't numbers, it's the numbers that are their names.

We've been visited by children who lost their mother, a husband who lost his wife, a mother who lost her son, a boy of Keira's age: the mother of little Mustafa R.

Practically all that's left of Mustafa R. is his mother, I tell Lucas one evening when Keira is already asleep. Lucas knows that he has to spend time with me and listen when I need it. He knows that my job isn't just any job, he knows that each day is etched into me like a tiny wound transmitted to me from others. I haven't grown numb like a doctor, I'm not immune to kidnappings and torture and murders.

Who's Mustafa R.? asks Lucas, handing me a glass of red wine.

Mustafa R. is a boy from Srebrenica of whom practically nothing is left. On the last morning of his life he dawdled before school: he played too long in his room for starters and was then told by his mother to go brush his teeth. When she came to the bathroom to check on him a little later, she caught him playing with her facial cream. Riled up, she told him to leave her cream alone. *Leave my cream alone!* is what she said.

Mustafa never returned from school. As if he'd vanished into thin air. On that same day his mother had to flee, all townspeople had to flee because they were threatened with guns, blows, and kicks. All she took along was a small travel case and a vinyl bag.

We told Mustafa R.'s mother, when she came to us, to bring us something that could help us find her son. *I've nothing but his name*, she said. But a couple of days later she returned, saying, *This is the only thing I have left.*

The only thing was a negative: all that had remained to Mustafa R.'s mother was his fingerprint left in the jar of facial cream, which she'd fortunately never used again to preserve her boy's memory.

The son was found in a pit near Zvornik. We restored to his skeleton the name that would have otherwise remained imprinted in a jar of cosmetic cream.

A grim story, said Lucas, gazing away through the window. *I think we ought to get back to the UK, all this is too hard for you. Think about it, is it worthwhile to extend the contract?*

My contract expires in four months, next week at the latest I'll have to extend it or else notify London that we're coming home. My work here is harder than I'd expected, it's destroying my psyche. I'm ridden by nightmares, Lucas says that I ought to spend more time with Keira and that I'm quieter than usual. But I must hold out, I must help those people.

On this extended weekend we're planning a low-cost flight to our London home. We're going to visit my mom and Lucas's parents, Keira's going to get together with her pals, it's a packed schedule for three days. On Thursday I lock the computer files I've been using at work with a triple password, go home and start packing; again I catch myself thinking gloomy thoughts as I stash my facial cream in my toiletry bag. *Against wrinkles*, it says. Against wrinkles means against the years, against the years means against time, against time means against life. There's nothing that cosmetics can conceal or smooth out, only their packaging is useful for children's fingerprints.

Then I think of the creature in the vase, whose water my folks have been conscientiously changing ever since her discovery. She must go away because she might turn into a small slimy monster in our absence. An idea occurs to me: what if I secretly flushed the water from the vase down the toilet and the creature mysteriously vanished? I'd tell Keira that she must have croaked her way out of her living space and hopped through the window. But I couldn't pull off such a lie and Keira is no longer a little girl to fall for every fib.

That varmint, ahem . . . the creature, I correct myself, *what do we do with it?*

You mean Olivija? asks Lucas.

What about Olivija? Keira tenses up.

Lucas says that she'll survive three days without us because she eats bamboo roots and that we can leave her where she is.

And if she develops in the meantime? If she turns into a recognizable animal and we find her sitting in the middle of the rug when we come back? She's half an inch long already, and growing at light speed.

Lucas and Keira are eyeing me mistrustfully.

That creature, that . . . Olivija—she must go! I remain adamant.

Keira bursts into tears and Lucas hugs her. I'm the evil mother on the bank of the river in which an innocent little critter is swimming, and on the opposite bank is the bitter crying of an injured child. I glower at Lucas who ought to side with me, together we ought to convince the child that there's no point in upholding the holiness of life at all costs and in such extreme cases.

All right, it dawns on me at last. *We'll make a compromise.*

On Friday morning we eat breakfast at the crack of dawn, hastily clear the table, zip the last travel bags, and get dressed. Buttoning up her coat, Keira runs to the windowsill and grasps the vase, cupping it carefully. We make our way downstairs; Keira is treading warily while the bamboo in the vase is jittering to the rhythm of her footsteps. On stepping from our Sarajevo house we can see that our cab's already waiting. Setting down our luggage, we wave at the cab driver to signal that we'll be back in a moment, and turn left toward our yard. Lucas pushes the foliage aside and Keira sets the vase in a spot where it's hidden from sight when Lucas lets the bush branches drop back. Now Olivija can go on swimming undisturbed, everyone's happy . . . anything to keep Keira from moping.

Arriving at the airport, we queue up for the London flight. I've solved nothing, I reflect through the echoes of the loud-speaker announcements, all I'm doing is backing away from the problems for a couple of days, but once we're back I'll have to face an even bigger Olivija and all those ghosts that have names after all.

After check-in, there's still an hour left to kill before our flight.

Shall we go for a last kahva? Lucas asks jokingly.

The Rex

For my darling Tita

THE DEAFNESS OF THE depths is gobbling up the gloaming over-grown with velvety algae, gobbling it up till from the bottom there barely glimmers a hint of the carcass of an enormous brute, huge like a whale and hardened like a coral reef. For the sea-dust strewn corpse, its numbed timelessness began on September 12, 1944, four burning days after the Allied air raid.

*

Deafness, stillness and silence were things unbearable to Mr. Toscanini. But he was delighted with the pell-mell on the ocean liner: delighted with the strollers on the deck, bathers in the pool, young girls resting on striped folding chairs under sun-shades, staff running here and there, children playing in the ship playground. Mr. Toscanini, a waiter approached him discreetly, *the captain would like to invite you to dine at his table tonight, together with Miss Isa Miranda, the famous racing driver Nuvolari, and the boxer Primo Carnera.* Mr. Toscanini slightly nodded in agreement and sauntered away to watch the life on the deck again.

Slowness, clumsiness, and languor were character traits unbearable to Tazio Nuvolari. He was nettled because he'd come to dinner too early, thus missing the chance of having his fellow diners rise and bow to him on arrival. Sulkily he ordered a gin-and-soda, which he drank only on such rare occasions as the present, when he didn't have to set foot in a car for three weeks.

He noticed an approaching beauty of about thirty, accompanied by a younger woman. Wasn't it that actress, Mirella, Miradina, Miranda . . .

Arrogance, haughtiness, and conceit were features unbearable in men to Isa Miranda. As soon as she noticed Nuvolari's searching, supercilious look dissecting her from toe to head, she raised her chin somewhat. Just before she reached the table, Nuvolari, who had speed in his blood, sprang to his feet, said, *Allow me, Tazio Nuvolari*, darted to her prospective chair and helped her sit down. Recognizing the famous racing driver, Isa Miranda brightened up, offered him her hand to kiss and sat down. *What brought you to America, a race maybe?* the actress wondered politely, but her question was never answered because just then an elderly gentleman, Mr. Toscanini, approached the table in the captain's company and a moment later came hurrying the great boxer, Primo Carnera, the captain introduced the guests and the dinner could begin.

As early as the aperitif, a glass of bitters from the ship cellar, Nuvolari wanted to know how fast they were sailing. *Our current speed is twenty-six knots*, replied the captain, *I'm sorry to say we no longer hold the Blue Riband, we earned it in '33 when we covered the distance between Gibraltar and New York in four days, thirteen hours and fifty-eight seconds, at an average speed of twenty-nine knots.* The actress, the youngest guest at the celebrities' table, wondered what a blue riband was. *It's a twenty-nine-meter banner, a meter earned for each knot, our ship held it for two years: before us it flew on the German ship,* Bremen, *and after us it was sported by the Atlantic liner,* Normandie.—*But isn't it dangerous—this speed, I mean?* wondered Mr. Toscanini. *Speed, speed, that's the biggest thrill of all, if you haven't known the shivers of speed down your spine and the wind rushing past your ears, you've missed a lot*, Nuvolari warmed up, *and it makes no difference if it's a Bugatti, Bianchi, Ferrari, Maserati, or Porsche.*

The waiters served the *hors d'oeuvre*, prawns in wine sauce,

and deftly whirled away. The guests were chatting, only Carnera
the boxer was completely quiet. *All this speed*, Mr. Toscanini
was shaking his head, *time is money, sure, but why all the rush?
Make haste slowly, that's what old people used to say.—Who are
you talking to?* retorted Tazio Nuvolari, whispered something in
the waiter's ear, and the waiter returned in fifteen minutes with
a small crate of wood. Carefully, Nuvolari took off the lid, and
what his neighbors at the table glimpsed first was a large lettuce
leaf, but when he pushed aside that too, they saw a gilded turtle
with the initials TN imprinted into the shell. *Years ago it was
presented to me by none other than the poet Gabriele D'Annunzio,
and his words were: "The slowest animal for the fastest human." I
never go anywhere without it, I've even had the image of a turtle
with my initials printed on my competition shirts and stationery
and painted on my airplane.—You have an airplane?* blurted Isa
Miranda, regretting her child's surprise the very next moment.
*Sure, but when it comes to crossing the Atlantic I've more faith in
the Rex*, laughed Nuvolari, and everyone smiled but the boxer,
Primo Carnera, who remained grave, staring silently at his plate.

D'Annunzio and those, what-d'you-call-them, Futurists, continued Mr. Toscanini while the main course was being served,
aren't they speed worshippers, too?—Of course, answered the driver,
*they are, I know them, I know lots of people, seven years ago I was
received by the Duce himself at the Villa Torlonia, we even had
a picture of us taken together behind the wheel of the Alfa Romeo
P3 number eight, and, speaking of Mussolini, did you know that
he wanted to rechristen the Rex as the Dux* . . . Crimson-faced,
Mr. Toscanini excused himself and rose from the table, while
the others went on picking at their—very palatable—seabream.

*And you, Miss Isa, might I ask whether you were overseas on
business or pleasure?* asked the captain. *On business, fortunately,
they wanted me in Hollywood, we were shooting a new movie,
Hotel Imperial, directed by Robert Florey, Ray Milland's on the
cast, too*, answered Isa Miranda, *but it's not supposed to reach the
movie theaters for a good year yet*. Nuvolari was jousting with his

fish, the famous conductor was gone and there fell an indecorous silence, broken by the captain: *In short, it's an honor for us to dine with the new Marlene Dietrich,* he paid her a compliment.

Mr. Toscanini didn't come back before the dessert and the captain, guessing the cause of his absence, was beginning to worry, but the conductor calmed him down with a meaningful look. *If you don't like speed, do you like slowness then?* the driver harped on. *Nimble, deft slowness,* replied the musician, *not rigid or monotonous. You've told us about your emblem, well, there are emblems in humanist books bearing the caption "Make haste slowly," and you'll find among them a dolphin wound around an anchor or a butterfly paired with a crab,* he added. Isa Miranda wondered what those animals were supposed to symbolize. *The light, nimble butterfly with the slow but persistent crab, now isn't that an inventive combination,* said the captain, beckoning to the waiter.

Where are you in such a rush to get to? asked Mr. Toscanini. *Nowhere, that's the whole point, I don't race because I'm in a hurry but for pleasure,* replied Nuvolari. *If everyone hurried like you,* the old gentleman stood his ground, *they'd be dead by now, they'd have rushed straight to death, books would be at least one tenth shorter because the story could be told without descriptions, detailed explanations, or digressions, compositions would be played out in five minutes, we'd have nothing left to focus on, I hope that it won't happen for a long time to come. Can't you see, Mr. Tazio, that there's a pleasure in delaying, too, in savoring a vanishing moment, Verweile doch, du bist so schön . . .* Carnera looked surprised and went on—or perhaps resumed—keeping silent, like the turtle, which was clambering in its crate by the foot of the table.

The captain invited his illustrious guests to the ship's veranda for coffee. *The Rex is eight years old, she was built in 1931 in Genova,* he explained, sipping from a Rosenthal porcelain cup, *and christened by King Victor Emmanuel and Queen Elena. She has two powerful engines with one hundred forty thousand horse-power, twelve exhaust pipes channeled into those two smokestacks rising fifteen meters above the deck, with two sirens, and there are two masts as well, as you will have noticed, both forty-five meters high. And we have twenty-four lifeboats. The ship measures two hundred and seventy meters in length, thirty in breadth and forty in height.—How many of us are there on board?* asked Mr. Toscanini. *We have eight hundred and seventy crew members and over two thousand passengers*, replied the captain. *Splendid, splendid*, Nuvolari enthused, *a fast brute, this queen of ships, and she runs as smooth as clockwork, too.—Certainly, certainly, but there was some trouble with the engines at her first launch, well, I don't want to alarm you, and she had to stop at Gibraltar to have them fixed*, continued the captain. *Some passengers were so frightened that they disembarked and continued by another boat, and didn't their eyes just pop out to see the Rex already moored in New York when they arrived*, said the ship's commander proudly, stroking his beard. *The pride of our navy, this quick beastie*, commented Nuvolari, *oh yes, quick beastie . . . now where is it, where have I left—oh dear, I've forgotten my turtle in the dining room, hey, waiter, look sharp, the turtle in the crate, bring it here, hurry up!*

As throughout that evening, the conqueror of the world's boxing rings, Primo Carnera, never gave a peep even ten minutes after the waiter's return. What is more, he remained unruffled by Nuvolari's piercing scream at the news that the waiter had not found the turtle. The crate certainly: that he brought back, to the relief of its owner. But his satisfaction lasted for the mere twinkling of an eye. When he raised the lid, there was nothing inside but the lettuce leaf and shredded bedding.

Mobilized were almost all of the four hundred and fifty waiters, a third of the two hundred and sixty sailors, some telegraphers and telephone operators. The turtle was sought all over the twelve stories of the liner, in the first, special, third, and tourist classes (there was no second class because no one would have wanted to travel in it), it was sought in the movie hall, theater, bank, library, physiotherapy department, and photographer's studio; in the ship's stores, barbershops, beauty salons, kitchens, restaurants, bars, and offices; in the elevators, the children's playground, the gallery, chapel, gym—the largest room on board—and even the printing press which published the paper *Sea News*. A sailor was ordered to jump into the swimming pool and search it thoroughly, although the staff was strictly forbidden to bathe there. *Missing is a turtle with a gilded shell and the initials TN, tee en, if you have any information about it, please report to the administration or communicate the details to a crew member without delay*, the loudspeakers blared on and below the deck of the ocean liner. Tazio Nuvolari suffered agonies. First he headed for the dining room and combed it thoroughly, then returned to the veranda, nervously pacing to and fro. *I do hope it's found*, Isa Miranda told him later in the evening and took her leave, soon to be followed by Mr. Toscanini and Primo Carnera, who returned to their respective cabins.

Later, Nuvolari was visited in his cabin by the captain. *It hasn't been found yet*, lashed out his bluff announcement. *Didn't you think that the boxer was a little odd?* asked the driver. *I mean, he kept mum all the time, never said a word, a guy like him's bound to have a trick up his sleeve, what do you say?*—*Maybe he's just a close, uncommunicative character, a bit shy perhaps*, the captain tried to clear Carnera, for it would hardly do for the supreme commander of a ship to blacken a passenger's name, least of all a celebrity's. *Shy—a boxer? Give me a break . . . what about that old Toscani?* Nuvolari went on drilling. *Toscanini*, the captain corrected him, *surely you don't think that your pet could have been stolen by the famous conductor, he's certainly got better things to do in life.*—*Sure, sure*, said Nuvolari, *but do you remember how he suddenly flushed and legged it from the table without excusing himself, and then never showed up for the longest time?*—*Well, yes, but that was for a different reason, at least I think so*, the seaman struck a conciliatory tone again, *but I'm telling you this in strict confidentiality, I'm counting on your discretion: he didn't like your*

*references to those modern writers, let alone the Duce.—What, not
like the Duce? The man doesn't even know him*, the sportsman
flared up. *He's an opponent of the régime*, continued the captain,
*it's unusual that he's traveling by an Italian ship at all, and as he
refuses to set foot on his native soil, he's going to board a barge at
landing, it will pick him up by the ship's side and take him to the
Yugoslav coast, from where he's traveling to Salzburg. But let it rest
for now, as soon as anything comes to light you will be apprised*, the
ship's commander tried to take his leave. *Wait a moment, what
about that actress, Mirandolina, you know how snottily she looked
at me when she came to the table, she didn't take to me either, at
least not at first, later she mellowed all right.* But the idea of her
filching the gilded turtle struck the captain as simply impossible.

After his departure Nuvolari stonily huddled in his cabin.
Motionless like a sea cliff, quite unlike the racer he was, he sat
on his bed and stared at the empty crate all night and the next
morning and the next afternoon, never touching a single dish
that was brought to his bedroom. But the next evening a cabin
boy knocked on his door, delivering a letter with the following
contents:

Esteemed Mr. Nuvolari,

*Perhaps all things on earth, even the dark and distressing ones,
have a purpose, and the disappearance of an endearing little animal
may allow you to take the time and reflect on your doings—no
innuendo intended, of course: to halt your body for a while, stop
your steel machine, and rev up the machine in your head instead.*

*You're hurrying, Nuvolari, to write your name in eternity, at
the highest possible speed you're heading for immobility. But in
eternity you will have to wind down, forever. Think of everything
that's now slipping from your hands, of the time that's relentlessly
draining away. You won't catch it by grasping for the future, it will
always outrun you. In our haste we have no time for nostalgia, let
alone love. Instead of serenely diving into the depths of the sea and*

exploring their treasures, we skim over the surface. But enough of this cheap moralizing, Nuvolari, you must be sick and tired of me!

Have you ever considered how drawn out human life is and how many days are empty? Somebody said once: How many people long for immortality but are flummoxed when it comes to spending a Sunday afternoon. And have you ever considered how personal the passage of time is in human life?

Look at the story of your own ocean crossing. One could simply say: Nuvolari embarked on such and such a day in 1937 on the Atlantic liner The Rex, and some days later, after dinner with the captain and several fellow celebrities, his turtle disappeared. Then the end of the story would follow, let us say: The turtle was found in such and such a place, or the turtle was never found. Pure boredom. (Although I admit that there are things that have to be told concisely.)

Alternatively, your voyage could be presented in quite a different light. Like this: Mr. Tazio Nuvolari, the renowned driver and winner of many a prize in speed racing, embarked one glorious sunny day in New York, the year 1937 it was, on one of the most famous Atlantic liners of the time, The Rex, which had once boasted the Blue Riband. And so on and so on and so on, making the reader or listener squirm with curiosity: Was the turtle found at last or not? And if so, where? Who had stolen it, etcetera?

As you will have realized yourself, all this narration is nothing but procrastination. But procrastination can be beautiful and pleasing. You, by contrast, are only interested in the ending. What lies at the end of the trot? Pause, dénouement, a new beginning? Well, I've tantalized you enough: your little turtle is safe and sound, chewing on a dry fig right now, and when you've read this letter, or rather skimmed through it (which seems more in your style), come to Cabin 12 to pick it up.

Who am I? Neither conductor Toscanini nor the stout boxer, Carnera. Nor am I comely Miranda. With this life rushing so fast, I hardly know myself who I am. Perhaps I'm nothing but the commander of a great lumbering brute, one of the fastest in the world. In fact I'm a great deal like you because I, too, hurry overmuch, but where I differ from you is in my longing for slowness.

Please do not be offended by my tasteless prank or repellent lesson. The theft of your pet was not planned, it simply happened of its own accord after yesterday's dinner. When I saw you rise and head for the veranda, I told the waiter to remove it to a safe place. My purpose was to check and curb time, yours and mine and everyone's, just for a split second.

Respectful greetings from
Your captain Giorgio C. Scotti

Enraged, Tazio Nuvolari folded the letter and dashed down the corridor in the direction where he expected to find Cabin 12. Storming across the deck toward the stem, he tore the captain's letter to pieces and tossed the scraps of writing across the rail, sending them down, swirling, to the sea surface.

And what happened next? Did Nuvolari box the captain's ears and challenge him to a duel? Or did he simply ignore the captain till the end of the voyage? Did he report the theft to the authorities on landing in Italy? We will learn about that a little later, for what was of interest were not only the events on the ship but under it as well. For a moment, then—just a figure of speech—we have to turn our backs on the events on board, to rein in or curb that time, as the captain would have said, and start rolling the time on the sea surface.

For that was where the maestro's camera was pointed: to the boats under the giant steamboat where Gradisca and her fellow townsmen were sitting. But take it slowly, as Maestro Fellini would have said, he knew how to develop this sequence in an appropriate rhythm, delaying but never tedious, with an Amarcord-tinted expectation, thus letting us know that a surprise lay in store for us at the end, and indeed, everything is like a child's magical expectation of Santa Claus. *Where are all these people going? Where are all these people going?* is the rhetorical question of a shabbily dressed man in the movie, who is heading for the coast together with his fellow townspeople to embark on the boats, *I'd like to tell you but I can't, because it's all still up in the air*, he adds. *Today is a very important day for our town*, says someone else. For Rimini, left deserted that evening. In the boats there's drinking and singing, the blind man is playing a melancholy tune on the accordion. *It will weigh about two and a half times the weight of the Grand Hotel*, is someone's estimate, *Go thou, Queen of the Sea*, says another, *"Thou passeth, and thy destiny I shall follow in the waves, watching your glistening wake,"* quotes a third. The town idiot spins a tall tale about a dolphin which once leaned its head against the gunwale of his boat and said: *Mamma!* We hear all this, waiting with bated breath for the surprise. Even Gradisca the town beauty, with tears coursing down her cheeks, speaks up about her misfortune in love. Meanwhile the sky has turned red and then dark, stars have lit up on its vault. *How can they all stay in place up there with no bricks, lime, or foundations*, wonders a mason. The blind man's accordion dies away, the people fall asleep in their shells and then, then . . . Only then do pins of light glow from the darkness, myriad lights, a boy wakes up, *There it is, there it is*, he yells, the townspeople start from their sleep and there's a giant whale of a ship sailing by them, decorated like a Christmas tree with a string of sparkling lights running from smokestack to smokestack. People are waving at it, shouting *The Rex, hurray for The Rex, the greatest thing the régime ever built!* and the Mayor yells: *As the representative of the Podestà I wish you a safe journey! Long live Italy!* The surprise is no mere surprise but a good omen, a promise that their wishes will come true some day. Gradisca is passionately blowing kisses at the queenly liner as if she saw in it her future lover, everybody is united in a common joy, the expected surprise is bringing a new hope, even the blind accordion player must be hoping for something as he is frantically asking in the climax of the scene: *What's it like, what's it like?*

Ship time can start rolling again, Nuvolari, who had stopped in his tracks when hurrying across the deck, like a figure on a movie tape stuck in the projector, returns to a light trot but suddenly stops and flops down on a bench. Pressing his hand against his spleen, he says to himself, *I shouldn't have run so hard,* the pain stabbing in his left side. He gazes into the dark distance, at the black waves, *How I miss my wife and both kids,* he thinks and is overwhelmed by a staggering homesickness, even though the ship is already sailing along the Italian shore. Returning to his cabin, he sits down and takes the time to write a long, long letter to his family, although he knows that he will reach home before the letter does.

*

Seven years later the ship, once the fastest of all, raced to its death. On the morning of September 8, she was attacked by six English bombers of the South African Royal Air Force, and after three consecutive attacks she capsized, sinking into the shallow sea between Koper and Izola where she'd been brought from Trieste for concealment from the Allies. The remains of the wounded brute, once the nimblest of dolphins, continued to burn for four days, a layer of petroleum and machine oil spreading across the sea. Then silt covered up the frame of the exquisite corpse, which remained lying, motionless, in the deafness of the depths and in numbed timelessness.

The Life and Death of Silent Silvina

no
las palabras
no hacen el amor
hacen la ausencia

Alejandra Pizarnik,
En esta noche, en este mundo

IN A NUTSHELL: ALEJANDRA was in love with Silvina, who was married to Adolfo, and Adolfito flirted with Elena, who was the wife of Octavio. Not to mention Adolfo's illegitimate daughter and son.

But things were not so simple after all. Silvina had always felt that there was more to her than one person. Every time she entered her childhood bedroom, she was a different Silvina, bringing with her a new story, inner or outer, one she'd spun by herself or one that had happened to her in the so-called real life. With each arrival in the same room Silvina halved and multiplied, she was becoming her own copy, imitation, and replica in ever-new editions. Besides, there were a number of Silvinas for all the people she knew, and if they had all gathered to chat about her, they would have believed they were talking of different women. In one respect only was Silvina always the same: she never changed her attitude to any individual friend, and that was why she was regarded as consistent, self-assured, and upright.

Silvina fell in love with Adolfo when she was thirty and he was nineteen. Wearing white on that day, a tennis racket in hand, he already had all the features of the successful gallant that he was to become. As lovers in an unheard-of scandal, *him so young, and her practically an old maid!* they used to meet at her place, where she lived in comfort thanks to her parents' wealth, earning some extra money with working for a magazine and publishing her short stories. She wrote sonnets to him and perceived him through eyes that shut out all surrounding time and space. They married seven years later.

Then came years of gauzy happiness, friends, Jorge Luis whom they called Georgie, Julio and others, writing, reproaches, reviews, *Why didn't you come home last night?* the magazine, her sister Victoria, *Where were you all night?* the anthology, books, Adolfito, books . . . And then the Mexican encounter with Octavio and his wife Elena in Paris. They admire and praise each other. Elena is beautiful, young, and cheerful, showing an interest in everything. Including Adolfo. The paths of the couples split and Silvina heaves a sigh of relief into the stillness, an inaudible breath drifting from her mouth as she nearly exhales her whole soul into the soundless pampa, raising the tiny grains of orange sand.

Round came the years when some things were not talked about, that was the family policy, including the fact that Silvina would have loved to have a child, that she longed to give birth to something else besides written pages, but in the meanwhile time and pages piled up. Fourteen years after their wedding a crushed Adolfito came to tell her that a chambermaid in southern France, where he'd been a writer in residence, was going to give birth to his child, and in that instant another Silvina emerged from her form, locked herself in her room, cried out the damned eyes that had refused to see anything around him, anything beyond the contours of Adolfito's figure, and shut herself in discreet silence. All she told him was, *We'll raise your child as our own.*

She arranged everything for the adoption and they fetched the baby from France. Little Marta was the joy of her life and Silvina, in her new stepmother character, was rewarded by keeping Adolfito. She would flow and ebb from a child's prattle into poetry and fantastic short fiction, and back among the toddling words. Little Marta grew up among her mother's uneasy tales of children shut up in fairytale towers, children who painted with magical colors that made the pictures real while they themselves remained confined to the imagination. *Why does the little boy in the story stay in the imagination, Mama, why doesn't the story have a happy ending, so he could become real too?* About this Silvina kept her silence, her maternal instinct was appeased but she always hovered in a terrible uncertainty about what was right and wrong.

In the evenings she still lounged on a cushioned settee by the window from which she could best see when Adolfito came home.

When she heard that Mrs. Sara J. Demaria had given birth to her husband's baby, a boy named Fabián, she descended a step deeper into an ever more charged silence.

With her Sartre lips and butterfly glasses she walked through the streets of Buenos Aires, beautiful in her ugliness, her wavy hair falling on her forehead, she wandered all over Reina del Plata for two days to avoid talking. Where had he been last night, why hadn't he come home again? Then she returned and he gave her a sympathetic look. Sympathetic, yes, for she was his wife and co-author, they were creating an illusion together. So it was and he couldn't help it, he could change nothing, for he, too, was caught in God's patterns, he had to shatter himself into every molecule of this world if he was ever to depart in peace to the other.

Nothing changed, except that she began to wait for him in bed every night, and at the rattling of the key in the entrance door she quickly turned to the wall and feigned sleep. Nothing changed, except that she never spoke about the pain, that she accepted the noise around her and abstracted all other dimensions. Nothing changed, except that she noticed the growing number of letters from Paris, from the address Rue Victor Hugo 199, which was the residence of the Fair Elena, Octavio's wife.

Nothing changed, except that in '67 she met Alejandra at the home of Sara Facio, the photographer. It happened just a few days after Alejandra reviewed Silvina's book for the *Sur* magazine. Alejandra was thirty-one at the time. Silvina was sixty-four.

Silvina found herself in a double, uncomfortable mother role. Being of Russian origin, the short-haired Alejandra signed her letters to Silvina as Sasha. Those letters were overflowing with yearning and other pathetic baggage. But they were sincere, written in blood, *Sylvette ma très chère, it isn't the fault of the fever, I'm just endlessly grateful for your being so marvelous, such a genius.* The two shared a passion for painting and poetry, they shared despair and loneliness. The dead have bad dreams, the dead do not hear, the living are not going to hear, Alejandra wrote in one of her poems. Alejandra was a gloomy girl, wounded in the first-person singular, full of childhood complexes and meandering thoughts, which brazenly revealed to her and to the world that language was a lie and the rest was stillness, except that stillness didn't really exist. Perhaps she fell in love with Silvina because Silvina didn't know stillness but knew about silence. She multiplied Silvina in poems and letters, in tears and crises, words do not engender love, words create absence.

When Sasha and Silvina met, Adolfo had pursued an epistolary romance with Elena for eighteen years. He had sent her seventy-five letters, twelve telegrams, and two cards from all ends of the earth. Truth be told, they concerned not only love but literature as well. *Elena adorada, I was moved by your translation of my book*, he wrote, *it seems to be a good book in the foreign language, though you will now reveal the flaws in my writing and all the limitations of my mind.* To say more about the intimate contents of the letters would be highly indiscreet if an aging Elena hadn't sold them to the Princeton University Library herself.

What Elena revealed to the world, Silvina kept secret all her life. The seeming love pentangle was in fact a myriadangle, for Silvina was not one but a myriad Silvinas, a new one born with each stab of pain. And there may have been more than one Elena as well. For Silvina, to be sure, Elena did not exist: there was an Elena, wife to Octavio, but no Elena, love of Adolfito's life, who multiplied with each of Adolfo's letters, much after Silvina's own fashion, although idealized. One day the correspondence halted and Elena stopped shredding herself to paper. Being involved in an espionage scandal, she fled to Europe, but not before she quarreled with Adolfo, who was supposed to keep an eye on her cats yet let them run wild, on purpose or not. When love is to end, it doesn't choose its means.

Time and pages piled on and Silvina went on multiplying, she was losing words, meanings, glances, and voices, she no longer remembered who Adolfito was, or Octavio, or Elena, the only one she recognized from time to time was Marta, and in the deepest of dreams she might have sometimes seen Alejandra.

As if the game of make-believe were growing too demanding for its protagonists, the second half of the century or its close saw them drop out, one by one. The first to leave them all was Alejandra—whether with any proof of Silvina's potential love, she alone knows. Sashenka, who had written years before the famous line *I want to die*, crossed into another world in September 1972 with the aid of barbiturates.

Elena died a few months after Octavio. They had been divorced for forty years. Her last days were surrounded by a host of cats and cigarette smoke.

On the very eve of the millennium died Adolfito, the great Adolfo who had invented inventions, fantasized about the fantastic and loved love and the swish of the letter opener.

Somewhere between Alejandra and Octavio, Silvina Ocampo passed away, too. She fluttered away like the unbound pages of a book carried off by the wind, each page is a different Silvina and there are many of them, each page full of love, love for Adolfito, love for Marta, love for Adolfito, love for Alejandra, love for Adolfito, love for Elena, love for Adolfito . . . Perhaps she became the voice written all over in Alejandra's poem, *There's someone here who is trembling, it can't be your imaginary voice crawling across the floor?* But Silvina never crawls across floors, Silvina walks through gardens, barefoot and erect, singing lullabies to Marta, who died in a car accident three weeks after her death. Silvina sings in a voice lent to her by the great whisperer, Silvina sings, Silvina knows through whose gardens to pass.

Papilio Dardanus

THEY CALLED ME *MADAME* Butterfly but I never knew whether it was in surprise or mockery: they probably saw me as a daft scientist, wrapped in her little cocoon while important events went unnoticed under her very nose. But though there may be some parallels between the stories of Cho Cho San and myself, my own chapter promises to end much more prosily.

This is what I'm musing about here, in this deep trench, from which I'm watching clouds slowly retreat from twilight like dragonflies and moths, their wings growing rosy with the hue of the sunset. The west must be on my left because that's where the clouds are tinted, while the other side, presumably the eastern one, is already fading into gray, presaging darkness. That's all I can make out, I'm lying motionless because the right side of my body won't obey me, and I feel like a dying Laos butterfly: the first part to go numb is the pair of wings on one side, then on the other, and finally, slowly, the torso with the feelers dies away, too. Blades of grass are tickling my face and hands, but I have so little control over my body that I can't even brush them away.

It was a nasty fall: when I'd nearly caught a fine specimen of *Nymphalis antiopa*—how absurd that this butterfly should be called a "mourning cloak" in some Germanic languages—I took an awkward step and began to slide downhill the very next moment, then plummeted down here unconscious. My butterfly net is lying a bit further up, but I can't reach it and the two locals who accompanied me have disappeared; no wonder, since I'd paid for their services in advance. Those two Mexicans have certainly not gone for help and there's no point in fooling myself that someone will come and pick me up. They've left me here, discarded me like a dirty rag, a snotty European whom they milked for all they could, brushing guilty conscience away like an annoying moth.

They were recommended to me by a trusty-looking clerk at the hotel reception desk, and the very next day the two sun-tanned, mustached fellows stood in front of my door, listening docilely to my orders: take the leather case for the samples, the butterfly nets and the travel bag with the instruments and spare materials . . . They just stared at me in disbelief before they grasped what I wanted, and that I could only get through by gesticulating. Which included waving my arms in imitation of fluttering. I find it outrageous that today, in the 1940s, someone working in hostelry or tourism shouldn't understand English, just as I find it incomprehensible that one shouldn't aspire to knowledge; if I'm to be an entomologist, I should speak several languages and have at least some grasp of geography, not to mention the basics of physics and chemistry. One has to adapt to life as certain animals do: to survive at all, they adopt the form and color of other species that are inedible or dangerous. And with this we come to the fact that a lepidopterologist like myself should even be knowledgeable about theology and other creationist questions when, say, answering the question who had advised butterflies, the subjects of her research, to adorn their wings with painted eyespots, true works of art, and trick the enemy into thinking that those eyes belong to a larger animal: a cat, an owl, a lizard.

For my part, however, I've never wondered how to make myself invisible or uninteresting to others, how to show with my pattern that I can be toxic food, how to imitate the male form in order to survive as an independent woman traveler in this macho world. Mimicry comes to me naturally and spontaneously, I honed it to a skill after I met Khalil and learned the truth about him. I was his teacher of lepidopterology, he was my teacher of adaptation. A perfect couple.

He approached me one hot day in Petaloudes, the so-called Valley of Butterflies on Rhodes, with his broad smile and jaunty mustache—a dangling snake glued under his nose, as long as his lips. I can spot frauds at once and the shifty element didn't escape me, but there was an endearing boldness about him that kept me from turning him away at once and made me listen instead, it might have been his courageous, carefully shaven chin, his serene brow, perhaps his regal nose and his erect, tall stature. In fairly correct English with a heavy accent and sharp r's, he said that he'd always harbored an interest in insects but had been prevented from enrolling in entomology studies in Athens by the lack of money, he said he'd left behind in Damascus an even direr poverty than his current circumstances, he said he'd do anything I ordered him to do and that he had no qualms about obeying a woman, although he was a Syrian and a Muslim by birth, he said he'd do anything to work with butterflies and earn something to boot, though he might well consider it beneath himself, scion of the fallen Turkish-Syrian nobility that he was.

I gave him a chance and a distinguished place in my entourage: he became my first assistant, for the other three Greeks I'd hired could hardly be expected to do more than carry my equipment through the heat and dust or crawl through thickets, as quietly as possible so as not to alarm the finest specimens. The delicate part, however, belonged to Khalil: once I'd reassured myself that his hand was precise and reliable, and, to tell the truth, grown a little infatuated with his refined, almost aristocratic fingers, I entrusted to him the lepidopterologist's voodoo: impaling butterflies on pins. He did it with a particular relish, and for all his carefulness, as if he were unwilling to hurt a living creature, there was something sadistic in his manner that I refused to see or admit.

If I had to describe him, I'd say that his skin was the color of a *Papilio roxelana*'s wings, ochre yellow: like dusty light, a decadent complexion, like his native Syria in lazy sunlight. There was a solemnity about him as if he were always anticipating a performance, always sitting in the theater pit, in the subdued glow that endows the audience with such beauty and fascination as to make one wonder: Who are they, what has brought them to the theater, curiosity, passion, or vanity—the urge to keep up with the repertory and show off their best clothes? When I touched him once in those early days, more or less by accident if such a thing exists, he seemed delicate and crumbly, as if covered by microscopic particles—and the reason why a butterfly's wings must not be touched is precisely the risk of damage to the sensitive scales, they shouldn't even be brushed if the butterfly is to live long.

On Rhodes we looked for *Lemonia balcanica*, in Sicily for *Alucita acutata*, for several endemic species in the African jungle and for the tree nymph in Ceylon, we smuggled from Manila a crate of cigars, more for fun than in earnest, we were on Fiji, where we found an unknown specimen and sent it to the London Natural History Museum, we were in Australia, surviving an earthquake and the attack of two dingoes, we caught the glass-winged *Greta oto* in Cuba, where we were finally caught ourselves as well: circling, we finally found each other with our long feelers. It happened in the tent, and I can only hope that our companions noticed nothing on that warmest of nights, when clustering moths perched far away from the lights and the last remnant of my mistrust dissolved.

Suddenly, none of the things about him that used to exasperate me jarred me any longer: his slowness, his Syrian smell of stale vanilla, his horsey laugh and the guttural sounds of his language, everything mellowed down and turned to me, began to stroke me and please me, I too slowed down my eternal grasping for discoveries, surrendered and relaxed into a gentle drowsiness, almost a stupor. The butterfly counts not months but moments, and has time enough, Khalil quoted a thought by Tagore which he'd seen in the epigraph to one of my books, and at that time I didn't find it schmaltzy at all. Before us stretched our entire lives and the freedom of the whole world, we might go wherever we wanted, time and money were no obstacle; I was a rich heiress, my uncle had bequeathed to me and my sister a fortune that would have sufficed for my research journeys as long as I lived.

While Europe was being riven by war, we stayed where it was not felt, in Armenia and Turkey, exchanging the hum of airplanes for the silence of butterfly wings and for our quiet joint work, for our mute walks across tall grass meadows and our chase after Anatolian specimens. The only rustling came from my long skirt, the only smoke rising behind tall grass blades and tree trunks was the smoke puffing from his pipe, the only grating was heard from the pencil copying the patterns of the day's catch spread out—all the rest were other continents, cut off from our kitschy island.

He urgently had to go home, his mother had fallen seriously ill, he declared three months after the end of the war, but before leaving for Damascus some days later, he proposed to me. When I asked him why the sudden hurry, had he forgotten Tagore's thought on time, he waved it away and kissed me. He said, *I'll marry you as soon as I get back*. I never got round to asking whether he realized that I was a woman of modern principles and that I was not going to marry according to Muslim, Protestant, or—since we were in Greece at the time—Eastern Orthodox customs, and I never got round to looking inside myself to see whether I was still me, whether those were still my ideals of love and science: love sees a butterfly as a flying blossom while science sees it as an insect, admittedly pleasant to look at, interesting and worthy of study because it's equipped for pollination and capable of mimicry. Were those still my ideals of freedom or had I given in to the realization that I could never have met a more kindred soul, great cultural differences notwithstanding?

After his departure my days passed in solitude, I gathered butterfly eggs on trees and fostered them, sold a number of them to collectors and was bored to death, deprived of something I had not known before Khalil. I even missed his Muslim habits, for instance the way he would approach water by putting his left foot first (which I was beginning to do myself, out of nostalgia for him) and leaving it right foot first. I missed what I used to find intolerable, such as his thanking Allah every time he moved his bowels, for delivering him from filth and allowing him to relieve himself. I was changing into him, I tried to compensate for him by doubling and imitation, I, formerly a confirmed Briton.

My darling, he wrote, *mother is worse and we have no money for medicines.* Of course I sent him money at once.

Mother is better but we've run out of medicines again, he wrote after a while. Of course I sent him more money.

He was always promising to return soon. Then he complained that there was money for the medicines but he had no work or earnings. I sent still more money.

This went on for a year, and then I decided to surprise him. I was setting out into the unknown, even though I had his address and last name. The journey was long and tiring, by train and by boat, and as I had no private luggage bearers, it took time to arrange and organize everything. I arrived unannounced and soon found his district. The woman at the door assured me that nobody of that name lived there, and a man translated her words for me, evidently carefully and consistently.

Once again I went to the police and to the registrar's office. The address did match Khalil's name. I returned to his home but this time concealed myself in a vaulted niche by an old house opposite. I waited the whole morning in the dust of the passing carts. Then he came out. They came out, he and four women and six children: the women wore long galabeyas and had their hair covered, the children looked dirty and muddy. I hesitated: should I jump in front of him and embrace him, should I wait? Who were those half-veiled women? None looked old enough to be his mother. Had he donned their colors or had they taken their pattern from the male, as butterfly females do? And who the hell were those screaming children?

When two of the women and the children went their separate ways, Khalil stepped into a large building. Running after him, I found myself in a spacious indoor fish market, among crates of swordfish, anchovies, and anglers, in the din of arm-waving sellers who loudly advertised their wares, and in the crowd of haggling buyers. The people, men for the most part, were casting surprised glances at me, an unaccompanied woman.

How could Khalil have exchanged butterflies for stinking fish, the freedom of the air for the weight of water? I lost him in the crowd at first but then noticed him again. Resolutely marching up, I stopped to face him. He was the same as always and yet different. There was something not genuine about him, as if he had been copied by a skilled hand that had nevertheless slipped a little now and then.

He looked at me inquiringly as if he saw me for the first time. Really, Khalil, you're a past master of deception, I thought, why didn't I admit it to myself at the start? But all I said was:

Khalil . . .

Khalil? Did you know Khalil? he asked.

I stared at him and the world spun around me, the fish crates leaped to the ceiling and the people whirled around me. And for a while there was nothing more.

You passed out, the man told me while I was lying in bed in an unknown house, with one of the half-veiled women moistening my forehead with a rag.

People often mistake me for him, said the man. He explained that he was Khalil's twin brother, his name was Khalid. *You know, Khalil means "beautiful" and "a good friend," and Khalid means "eternal." There's truth in our names, neither of us has been false to their meanings.*

The mother of Khalid and Khalil had in fact caught typhoid fever over a year ago, passing it on to Khalil. The mother survived, Khalil died.

My grief was drowned for a while by the anger in me. *Khalil is gone. But he has left behind two wives and three children.* Khalid turned round and pointed at them. Apparently they didn't speak English, so they never even batted an eyelid at his glance. *Khalil spent the last years abroad, he was helping some scientist with research on butterflies,* Khalid explained, almost proud that he could pass this information to someone who didn't know it yet. *A rich English scientist, Khalil impaled butterflies on pins for him,* Khalid continued, *even though Khalil must have known very little about those critters, he'd learned a few things earlier from books, as an amateur, and some more later with practice.* He was a fishmonger; the brothers had inherited from their father a small fishmonger's store on the outskirts of Damascus but were doing poorly. *So Khalil went into the world looking for work, and had the good luck to land someone who was paying him for nonsensical fumbling and the last year even for medicines, though these weren't to be had in Syria anyway. Still, money always comes in handy. And who are you yourself?* he remembered to ask after this torrent of words.

I used to work for the English scientist, too, I lied.

Would you help me write a letter to the Brit in good English, as if it was Khalil writing, still alive, and ask for another tidy sum? he raised his eyebrows in encouragement, looking appealingly into my eyes.

I don't even know how I left the house of chatty Khalid and the women, who stood by the wall like shadows and rustled around the house. I didn't even know which I believed, Khalil's or Khalid's story, the front or the back of the butterfly's wings, the former's mimetic color or the latter's symmetrical drawings of the former's fake mirror eyes. Before I left, I wrote the letter to the imaginary Briton, of course, wrote it there, in that house of ghosts, to Khalid's dictation, joining in the game which was played secretly by one brother and openly by the other. Indeed, it seemed to me that Khalid's dictating voice imitated Khalil's. Instead of putting the addressee's first name, mine, before the last name, I wrote on the envelope Mr. instead of Ms. Perhaps the letter would arrive in Greece by the same boat as me.

Khalil and I had vowed to marry and to find at last the rare *Nymphalis antiopa*, nothing but this feat could accomplish our mission. But a game of make-believe makes anything possible and our game may continue someplace else, in other meadows, so the London Natural History Museum will have to wait for its specimen till another time, of which butterflies have plenty and more. And lying in this deep trench, I imagine that this is how it must feel to be old and infirm, no longer obeyed by one's body, and I make believe that I really am frail and lame, for I'm not going to see old age anyway.

I'll never be found here, in this deep trench, motionless, so I'm running no risks by playing the game Khalil taught me: I can play at mimicry, imitation of old age, which is uninteresting and unpalatable, it makes nobody's mouth water. Even though I feel more like an awkward caterpillar than a lithe cabbage butterfly, I'm now a *Papilio dardanus*, my favorite butterfly, a species where the female imitates the male because he can defend himself better against predators: I dye myself in the same browns and yellows, I curve and sharpen the tips of my wings in his image, so that no one will even look at me. I can decant myself into *Monsieur* Butterfly, Khalil, or an old woman who wants to be left alone to die. No longer am I counting the days and nights lying in this trench, all I'm counting is the hours of my imaginary old age.

Sixty Percent

MY SON IS ALL-PRESENT. He is here and there and above and below, but most of all he is in four places. Because there are secondary and primary pits, the head explains.

I'd tell him, my son, if he was standing here before me, *Run, my boy, run, your breath outscreams the horror of the forest whose edge witnessed the terrible story from a distance, run, you'll come to the territory under our control, run, may Allah help you, run, maybe a tree will toss you a golden fruit, a juicy apple to moisten your parched mouth, to send new vigor coursing through your veins.*

The primary pits are those they fell into, explains the head of the excavation group. The secondary pits are where they were reinterred, well, actually just carted there by diggers and trucks, together with the soil.

Don't look back, I'd tell my son if he was standing here before me, I'd take his hand and tell him, *Maybe they're after you, maybe they know you were just pretending, maybe they know you're alive and hurrying through the magic forest which enfolds you in black joy, run, your left shoe has practically no sole left, stones are hurting you, dried twigs are hacking into your foot but the pain is helping you because it's at least partly blotting out that scene in the clearing, run, run after the sun that keeps falling, falling, and when you catch up with it, you can ask why it allowed all that to happen and then ran away, somewhere below is the sea, it's there that the orangey ball sinks, run, run, my boy, to catch up.*

Why would anyone want to reinter them, it's just extra work?

I ask. The head of the group gives me an odd look. Because the primary pits were discovered by American satellites, ma'am.

I'm all at sea. What American satellites? What *is* a satellite, anyway? All I know is that I'd gently push my son into flight, *Run, my son, till you reach the sea, then the Drina Wolves won't get you in their clutches, better to be torn by sharp cliffs than tortured by Arkan's Tigers and twisted by the queen of death around her fingers and stretched on the rack of her hand, run, run, better vanish into a tree top or wizen into a root, better freeze into gnarled tree bark, elves will help you if they're kind, if there's any kind creature left in the world at all, pour yourself into a puddle, evaporate into a cloud, crystallize into the night air or just run, run, run . . .*

Satellites are machines, ma'am, that watch the earth from space. Earlier, for instance, they'd taken pictures of neat green grass in the area near Zvornik, and some months later they noticed that everything was dug up. That's suspicious.

He probably means that it's suspicious because something has been newly buried there.

Do you understand, ma'am?

I'm not sure. But how could they have lost pieces of my son on the way? And if we've got a primary and a secondary burial site, that makes only two pits. Now the remains of my son were found in four places and brought together. Four minus two makes two, two pits are still missing. Or have they found, say, two limbs in each?

When the Serbs saw the American satellite images they panicked, ma'am, you see, and started transporting the contents of the burial sites to different spots, to cover the traces.

All four pieces click together before my eyes and I tell my patched-up son who is missing a piece of the skull, his left hand and his right leg below the knee: *You're hearing pain already, you're feeling the roars, you're waiting for angels, you're singing death songs, you're crumpling the burial soil in hand, you're smelling the grave, the kabur, stop thinking, my boy, just run, run, you'll* come among good people, *Allah-birum*, God knows, you'll come among people with the sky and the sun and the moon in their eyes, among those who know nothing, those who have been spared, ask them nothing, they won't know the answers, just look at you in surprise and give you a forbearing smile, they'll say, *You're full of flies and mosquitoes and other bugs*, they'll say, *Clean yourself up, you can't enter our clean houses looking like this, our houses have never been sullied and you're covered with bees' blood and wasps' gall, wash up before you cross our thresholds, wash up so that you don't carry this vermin into our homes, go behind the house and wash away all the filth*, and you'll go behind the house and turn on the shower and take off your rags and scrub and scrub, and at last, still dirty, you'll shuffle before the people who still carry the sky and the sun and the moon in their eyes and admit that you're dirty forever, and they'll shake their heads saying, *You'd better go, we're afraid of that filth from the underworld, from the ahiret, we're afraid of you, better run!*

But why won't they bury him? Why must I press him to keep running even now when he's no more?

Those are the rules, ma'am, we have our orders.

I don't know if I can trust him, this head of the excavation group, *My son, better run or you'll get caught by those who did this to you, run, ahbab, friend, run*, will say the people who still carry the sky and the sun and the moon on their tongues, and you'll want to protest, *I wasn't in the underworld at all, I was in a clearing*, but you won't convince them and you'll start running again, with fresh breath you'll make your way south through Bosnia till you reach the sea in which the sun sets, till darkness falls, till aksham falls, till Satan comes, till Sheitan comes, and then you'll hear the tevhid, the prayer for the dead that's chanted only by women, for only they are left behind their husbands' outlines, and you, who were meant to go with them to the ahiret, you've escaped from the pile of their wilted limbs and are roaming the world like a phantom, still trampling this forest soil, run, run, you'll come to the river but not *even the river will cleanse you, it won't know how to wash out the past, save the present, ennoble the future, so you better run through this landscape, the legends are terrible, and watch out for mines too, or your story might be blown up.*

Those are the rules, we have orders to isolate the DNA first, and interment is allowed only when at least sixty percent of the skeleton has been assembled. No earlier.

Dee-en-ay . . . One percent is one part out of a hundred. How do I calculate how many percent they already have? How do I ask that? For me, my son is a thousand percent. *Don't believe anyone, my son, they'll tell you that there isn't enough of you to bury, they'll try to faze you with talk of how you'll be picked apart and your story chewed up by vermin, take your prayer beads with you, clasp the tesbih in your cut hands, clasp your fear, it may prove useful yet because you won't be able to tell this story, this story is true and truth can never be told, you know that well by now, when you come to the coast and the boundless sea is there and you wade in to wash, to clean away the clotted blood and scrub away all that caked dirt, there's smarting flesh pulsing underneath, it's being burnt by the sun, you have to find yourself a cave to hide in and block your ears from the chant of mourning women and chirping of insects, run, run, find a cave, somewhere far, far away.*

The head of the group for burial site excavation is giving me odd looks, but I know that my son is all-present, like God. He is here and there and above and below, but most of all he is present in four places in the earth, just as Allah is present in the four directions of the sky.

Born in 1967, VERONIKA SIMONITI's work has appeared in numerous international anthologies and has been translated into English, German, Croatian, Serbian, Italian, Hungarian, and Czech. Her first story collection, *Zasukane Storije* (*Twisted Stories*), received Slovenia's Best First Book of the Year in 2005. She published her second collection, *Hudicev jezik* (*The Devil's Tongue*), in 2011, and her first novel, *Kameno seme* (*The Stone Seed*), in 2014.

NADA GROŠELJ has contributed English translations to the bilingual editions of four Slovene Poets—Milan Jesih, France Preseren, and Tone Pavcek (with co-translators), and Joze Snoj—as well as to numerous anthologies. She translates from English, Latin, and Swedish into Slovene, and from Slovene into English.

MICHAL AJVAZ, *The Golden Age.*
The Other City.
PIERRE ALBERT-BIROT, *Grabinoulor.*
YUZ ALESHKOVSKY, *Kangaroo.*
SVETLANA ALEXIEVICH, *Voices from Chernobyl.*
FELIPE ALFAU, *Chromos.*
Locos.
JOAO ALMINO, *Enigmas of Spring.*
IVAN ÂNGELO, *The Celebration.*
The Tower of Glass.
ANTÓNIO LOBO ANTUNES, *Knowledge of Hell.*
The Splendor of Portugal.
ALAIN ARIAS-MISSON, *Theatre of Incest.*
JOHN ASHBERY & JAMES SCHUYLER, *A Nest of Ninnies.*
GABRIELA AVIGUR-ROTEM, *Heatwave and Crazy Birds.*
DJUNA BARNES, *Ladies Almanack.*
Ryder.
JOHN BARTH, *Letters.*
Sabbatical.
Collected Stories.
DONALD BARTHELME, *The King.*
Paradise.
SVETISLAV BASARA, *Chinese Letter.*
Fata Morgana.
In Search of the Grail.
MIQUEL BAUÇÀ, *The Siege in the Room.*
RENÉ BELLETTO, *Dying.*
MAREK BIENCZYK, *Transparency.*
ANDREI BITOV, *Pushkin House.*
ANDREJ BLATNIK, *You Do Understand.*
Law of Desire.
LOUIS PAUL BOON, *Chapel Road.*
My Little War.
Summer in Termuren.
ROGER BOYLAN, *Killoyle.*
IGNÁCIO DE LOYOLA BRANDÃO, *Anonymous Celebrity.*
Zero.
BRIGID BROPHY, *In Transit.*
The Prancing Novelist.

GABRIELLE BURTON, *Heartbreak Hotel.*
MICHEL BUTOR, *Degrees.*
Mobile.
G. CABRERA INFANTE, *Infante's Inferno.*
Three Trapped Tigers.
JULIETA CAMPOS, *The Fear of Losing Eurydice.*
ANNE CARSON, *Eros the Bittersweet.*
ORLY CASTEL-BLOOM, *Dolly City.*
LOUIS-FERDINAND CÉLINE, *North.*
Conversations with Professor Y.
London Bridge.
HUGO CHARTERIS, *The Tide Is Right.*
ERIC CHEVILLARD, *Demolishing Nisard.*
The Author and Me.
MARC CHOLODENKO, *Mordechai Schamz.*
EMILY HOLMES COLEMAN, *The Shutter of Snow.*
ERIC CHEVILLARD, *The Author and Me.*
LUIS CHITARRONI, *The No Variations.*
CH'OE YUN, *Mannequin.*
ROBERT COOVER, *A Night at the Movies.*
STANLEY CRAWFORD, *Log of the S.S.*
The Mrs Unguentine.
Some Instructions to My Wife.
RALPH CUSACK, *Cadenza.*
NICHOLAS DELBANCO, *Sherbrookes.*
The Count of Concord.
NIGEL DENNIS, *Cards of Identity.*
PETER DIMOCK, *A Short Rhetoric for Leaving the Family.*
ARIEL DORFMAN, *Konfidenz.*
COLEMAN DOWELL, *Island People.*
Too Much Flesh and Jabez.
RIKKI DUCORNET, *Phosphor in Dreamland.*
The Complete Butcher's Tales.
RIKKI DUCORNET (cont.), *The Jade Cabinet.*
The Fountains of Neptune.
WILLIAM EASTLAKE, *Castle Keep.*
Lyric of the Circle Heart.
JEAN ECHENOZ, *Chopin's Move.*

STANLEY ELKIN, *A Bad Man.*
The Dick Gibson Show.
The Franchiser.

FRANÇOIS EMMANUEL, *Invitation to
a Voyage.*

SALVADOR ESPRIU, *Ariadne in the
Grotesque Labyrinth.*

LESLIE A. FIEDLER, *Love and Death
in the American Novel.*

JUAN FILLOY, *Op Oloop.*

GUSTAVE FLAUBERT, *Bouvard and
Pécuchet.*

JON FOSSE, *Aliss at the Fire.*
Melancholy.
Trilogy.

FORD MADOX FORD, *The March of
Literature.*

MAX FRISCH, *I'm Not Stiller.*
Man in the Holocene.

CARLOS FUENTES, *Christopher Unborn.*
Distant Relations.
Terra Nostra.
Where the Air Is Clear.
Nietzsche on His Balcony.

WILLIAM GADDIS, JR., *The Recognitions.*
JR.

JANICE GALLOWAY, *Foreign Parts.*
The Trick Is to Keep Breathing.

WILLIAM H. GASS, *Life Sentences.*
The Tunnel.
The World Within the Word.
Willie Masters' Lonesome Wife.

GÉRARD GAVARRY, *Hoppla! 1 2 3.*

ETIENNE GILSON, *The Arts of the
Beautiful.*
Forms and Substances in the Arts.

C. S. GISCOMBE, *Giscome Road.*
Here.

DOUGLAS GLOVER, *Bad News
of the Heart.*

WITOLD GOMBROWICZ, *A Kind
of Testament.*

PAULO EMÍLIO SALES GOMES, *P's Three
Women.*

GEORGI GOSPODINOV, *Natural Novel.*

JUAN GOYTISOLO, *Juan the Landless.*
Makbara.
Marks of Identity.

JACK GREEN, *Fire the Bastards!*

JIŘÍ GRUŠA, *The Questionnaire.*

MELA HARTWIG, *Am I a Redundant
Human Being?*

JOHN HAWKES, *The Passion Artist.*
Whistlejacket.

ELIZABETH HEIGHWAY, ED.,
Contemporary Georgian Fiction.

AIDAN HIGGINS, *Balcony of Europe.*
Blind Man's Bluff.
Bornholm Night-Ferry.
Langrishe, Go Down.
Scenes from a Receding Past.

ALDOUS HUXLEY, *Antic Hay.*
Point Counter Point.
Those Barren Leaves.
Time Must Have a Stop.

JANG JUNG-IL, *When Adam Opens His Eyes*

DRAGO JANČAR, *The Tree with No Name.*
I Saw Her That Night.
Galley Slave.

MIKHEIL JAVAKHISHVILI, *Kvachi.*

GERT JONKE, *The Distant Sound.*
Homage to Czerny.
The System of Vienna.

JACQUES JOUET, *Mountain R.*
Savage.
Upstaged.

JUNG YOUNG-MOON, *A Contrived World.*

MIEKO KANAI, *The Word Book.*

YORAM KANIUK, *Life on Sandpaper.*

ZURAB KARUMIDZE, *Dagny.*

PABLO KATCHADJIAN, *What to Do.*

JOHN KELLY, *From Out of the City.*

HUGH KENNER, *Flaubert, Joyce
and Beckett: The Stoic Comedians.*
Joyce's Voices.

DANILO KIŠ, *The Attic.*
The Lute and the Scars.
Psalm 44.
A Tomb for Boris Davidovich.

ANITA KONKKA, *A Fool's Paradise.*

GEORGE KONRÁD, *The City Builder.*

TADEUSZ KONWICKI, *A Minor Apocalypse.*
The Polish Complex.

ELAINE KRAF, *The Princess of 72nd Street.*

JIM KRUSOE, *Iceland.*

AYSE KULIN, *Farewell: A Mansion in Occupied Istanbul.*

EMILIO LASCANO TEGUI, *On Elegance While Sleeping.*

ERIC LAURRENT, *Do Not Touch.*

VIOLETTE LEDUC, *La Bâtarde.*

LEE KI-HO, *At Least We Can Apologize.*

EDOUARD LEVÉ, *Autoportrait.*
Suicide.

MARIO LEVI, *Istanbul Was a Fairy Tale.*

DEBORAH LEVY, *Billy and Girl.*

JOSÉ LEZAMA LIMA, *Paradiso.*

OSMAN LINS, *Avalovara.*
The Queen of the Prisons of Greece.

ALF MACLOCHLAINN, *Out of Focus.*
Past Habitual.

RON LOEWINSOHN, *Magnetic Field(s).*

YURI LOTMAN, *Non-Memoirs.*

D. KEITH MANO, *Take Five.*

MINA LOY, *Stories and Essays of Mina Loy.*

MICHELINE AHARONIAN MARCOM, *The Mirror in the Well.*

BEN MARCUS, *The Age of Wire and String.*

WALLACE MARKFIELD, *Teitlebaum's Window.*
To an Early Grave.

DAVID MARKSON, *Reader's Block.*
Wittgenstein's Mistress.

CAROLE MASO, *AVA.*

HISAKI MATSUURA, *Triangle.*

LADISLAV MATEJKA & KRYSTYNA POMORSKA, EDS., *Readings in Russian Poetics: Formalist & Structuralist Views.*

HARRY MATHEWS, *Cigarettes.*
The Conversions.
The Human Country.
The Journalist.
My Life in CIA.

Singular Pleasures.
The Sinking of the Odradek Stadium.
Tlooth.

JOSEPH MCELROY, *Night Soul and Other Stories.*

ABDELWAHAB MEDDEB, *Talismano.*

GERHARD MEIER, *Isle of the Dead.*

HERMAN MELVILLE, *The Confidence-Man.*

AMANDA MICHALOPOULOU, *I'd Like.*

STEVEN MILLHAUSER, *The Barnum Museum.*
In the Penny Arcade.

RALPH J. MILLS, JR., *Essays on Poetry.*

CHRISTINE MONTALBETTI, *The Origin of Man.*
Western.

NICHOLAS MOSLEY, *Accident.*
Assassins.
Catastrophe Practice.
Hopeful Monsters.
Imago Bird.
Natalie Natalia.
Serpent.

WARREN MOTTE, *Fiction Now: The French Novel in the 21st Century.*
Oulipo: A Primer of Potential Literature.

GERALD MURNANE, *Barley Patch.*
Inland.

YVES NAVARRE, *Our Share of Time.*
Sweet Tooth.

DOROTHY NELSON, *In Night's City.*
Tar and Feathers.

WILFRIDO D. NOLLEDO, *But for the Lovers.*

BORIS A. NOVAK, *The Master of Insomnia.*

FLANN O'BRIEN, *At Swim-Two-Birds.*
The Best of Myles.
The Dalkey Archive.
The Hard Life.
The Poor Mouth.
The Third Policeman.

CLAUDE OLLIER, *The Mise-en-Scène.*
Wert and the Life Without End.

PATRIK OUŘEDNÍK, *Europeana.*
The Opportune Moment, 1855.

BORIS PAHOR, *Necropolis.*

FERNANDO DEL PASO, *News from the Empire.*
Palinuro of Mexico.

ROBERT PINGET, *The Inquisitory.*
Mahu or The Material.
Trio.

MANUEL PUIG, *Betrayed by Rita Hayworth.*
The Buenos Aires Affair.
Heartbreak Tango.

RAYMOND QUENEAU, *The Last Days.*
Odile.
Pierrot Mon Ami.
Saint Glinglin.

ANN QUIN, *Berg.*
Passages.
Three.
Tripticks.

ISHMAEL REED, *The Free-Lance Pallbearers.*
The Last Days of Louisiana Red.
Ishmael Reed: The Plays.
Juice!
The Terrible Threes.
The Terrible Twos.
Yellow Back Radio Broke-Down.

RAINER MARIA RILKE,
The Notebooks of Malte Laurids Brigge.

JULIÁN RÍOS, *The House of Ulysses.*
Larva: A Midsummer Night's Babel.
Poundemonium.

ALAIN ROBBE-GRILLET, *Project for a Revolution in New York.*
A Sentimental Novel.

AUGUSTO ROA BASTOS, *I the Supreme.*

DANIËL ROBBERECHTS, *Arriving in Avignon.*

JEAN ROLIN, *The Explosion of the Radiator Hose.*

OLIVIER ROLIN, *Hotel Crystal.*

ALIX CLEO ROUBAUD, *Alix's Journal.*

JACQUES ROUBAUD, *The Form of a City Changes Faster, Alas, Than the Human Heart.*

The Great Fire of London.
Hortense in Exile.
Hortense Is Abducted.
Mathematics: The Plurality of Worlds of Lewis.
Some Thing Black.

RAYMOND ROUSSEL, *Impressions of Africa.*

VEDRANA RUDAN, *Night.*

GERMAN SADULAEV, *The Maya Pill.*

TOMAŽ ŠALAMUN, *Soy Realidad.*

LYDIE SALVAYRE, *The Company of Ghosts.*

LUIS RAFAEL SÁNCHEZ, *Macho Camacho's Beat.*

SEVERO SARDUY, *Cobra & Maitreya.*

NATHALIE SARRAUTE, *Do You Hear Them?*
Martereau.
The Planetarium.

STIG SÆTERBAKKEN, *Siamese.*
Self-Control.
Through the Night.

ARNO SCHMIDT, *Collected Novellas.*
Collected Stories.
Nobodaddy's Children.
Two Novels.

ASAF SCHURR, *Motti.*

GAIL SCOTT, *My Paris.*

JUNE AKERS SEESE,
Is This What Other Women Feel Too?

BERNARD SHARE, *Inish.*
Transit.

VIKTOR SHKLOVSKY, *Bowstring.*
Literature and Cinematography.
Theory of Prose.
Third Factory.
Zoo, or Letters Not about Love.

PIERRE SINIAC, *The Collaborators.*

KJERSTI A. SKOMSVOLD,
The Faster I Walk, the Smaller I Am.

JOSEF ŠKVORECKÝ, *The Engineer of Human Souls.*

GILBERT SORRENTINO, *Aberration of Starlight.*
Blue Pastoral.
Crystal Vision.

Imaginative Qualities of Actual Things.
Mulligan Stew.
Red the Fiend.
Steelwork.
Under the Shadow.
ANDRZEJ STASIUK, *Dukla.*
Fado.
GERTRUDE STEIN, *The Making of Americans.*
A Novel of Thank You.
PIOTR SZEWC, *Annihilation.*
GONÇALO M. TAVARES, *A Man: Klaus Klump.*
Jerusalem.
Learning to Pray in the Age of Technique.
LUCIAN DAN TEODOROVICI, *Our Circus Presents . . .*
NIKANOR TERATOLOGEN, *Assisted Living.*
STEFAN THEMERSON, *Hobson's Island.*
The Mystery of the Sardine.
Tom Harris.
JOHN TOOMEY, *Sleepwalker.*
Huddleston Road.
Slipping.
DUMITRU TSEPENEAG, *Hotel Europa.*
The Necessary Marriage.
Pigeon Post.
Vain Art of the Fugue.
La Belle Roumaine.
Waiting: Stories.
ESTHER TUSQUETS, *Stranded.*
DUBRAVKA UGRESIC, *Lend Me Your Character.*
Thank You for Not Reading.
TOR ULVEN, *Replacement.*
MATI UNT, *Brecht at Night.*
Diary of a Blood Donor.
Things in the Night.
ÁLVARO URIBE & OLIVIA SEARS, EDS., *Best of Contemporary Mexican Fiction.*
ELOY URROZ, *Friction.*
The Obstacles.
LUISA VALENZUELA, *Dark Desires and the Others.*
He Who Searches.

PAUL VERHAEGHEN, *Omega Minor.*
BORIS VIAN, *Heartsnatcher.*
TOOMAS VINT, *An Unending Landscape.*
ORNELA VORPSI, *The Country Where No One Ever Dies.*
AUSTRYN WAINHOUSE, *Hedyphagetica.*
MARKUS WERNER, *Cold Shoulder.*
Zundel's Exit.
CURTIS WHITE, *The Idea of Home.*
Memories of My Father Watching TV.
Requiem.
DIANE WILLIAMS,
Excitability: Selected Stories.
DOUGLAS WOOLF, *Wall to Wall.*
Ya! & John-Juan.
JAY WRIGHT, *Polynomials and Pollen.*
The Presentable Art of Reading Absence.
PHILIP WYLIE, *Generation of Vipers.*
MARGUERITE YOUNG, *Angel in the Forest.*
Miss MacIntosh, My Darling.
REYOUNG, *Unbabbling.*
ZORAN ŽIVKOVIĆ , *Hidden Camera.*
LOUIS ZUKOFSKY, *Collected Fiction.*
VITOMIL ZUPAN, *Minuet for Guitar.*
SCOTT ZWIREN, *God Head.*

AND MORE . . .

FOR A FULL LIST OF PUBLICATIONS, VISIT: www.dalkeyarchive.com